THE GREAT SAUGATUCK MURDER MYSTERY

G Corwin Stoppel

❖

Lord Hiltensweiller Press

*In honour of my beloved wife and
partner in mischief and fun,
Patricia Dewey*

AT THE SAND BAR NOT SO LONG AGO

Bill wanted to close the Sandbar early that night. There was never much business on a Tuesday, especially a Tuesday after Labor Day had come and gone, and this evening wasn't any different. The rain didn't help much, either. He'd already sent Nick home. No point in having two bartenders for a small crowd of regulars, and not a tourist in sight out on the streets. Most of the regulars had already packed it in and gone home, leaving just Hack, the old retired navy chef and probably the best bookie in the area, still sitting at the bar. As always, three seats from the left end, his hat on the stool next to him, nursing the same beer he'd bought over an hour ago, studying his racing forms, same as he did every night. From time to time he'd look up, hoping someone had come in wanting to put some money on a horse running the next day at the track in Muskegon.

Aside from Bill and Hack, only Thomas and Al were still hanging on, sitting up near the front window on Butler Street, playing their guitars for the crowds that weren't coming. Bill would have closed up, but Old Chris usually came down from his apartment about this time for a shot of house whiskey, poured by Bill at less than cost. He'd stay open at least that much longer.

"Couple more tunes, fellows, and then let's call it a night. Business is slow," Bill told them. "Real slow," he said just under his breath.

Just as always, Chris came through the back door and perched on his favorite stool, two down from Hack. Bill reached for a glass and filled it, put it on the bar and scooped up four quarters.

"Got a new one I want you to hear," Thomas said. "I call her 'Big Lake.'"

"Go for it, Tommy," Bill said, hoping it might be a lively one. It was another ballad, but the refrain was catchy. Maybe the fellows could get this one on a CD and have it played on the radio. They'd been waiting for their big break for a long time.

"I was the first one to see her," Old Chris said over the music, staring down at his drink.

"And just who might that have been?" Hack asked, folding his paper, glad for anyone to talk to, even if Old Chris was wasn't exactly the betting type.

"The steamer. The *Aurora*. Prettiest steamboat I ever saw. Elegant, pretty. White wood, polished teak deck. She was an old one. Two big stacks pumping out the smoke, and a pair of big side wheels. Big Lake. That's what me think of her. I was the first to see her."

"When was that?" Billy asked.

"Must have been back in the summer of 1928. Yeah, summer of 1928, Venetian Week End. That's when I saw her. "Course Venetian Night back them aint what she's like now. It's better than it used to be, but that's when I saw her."

"How come you're so sure?" Bill asked, leaning over the bar to reach for the ash tray.

"On account of the fact that it was the first year I was out on the lake, working for my uncle on his fishing boat. Tweety was working for my uncle, too, when he was feeling all right. You remember him, don't ya? Got my papers the next year. So, that's why I know it was the summer of '28. And I know it was Venetian Week because that's when the murder happened. And I was the first to see her, and then tells Tweety. The *Aurora*. Prettiest boat I ever saw. A real looker, for sure. There aren't many of them left now days; weren't many left even back then. A real looker, for sure."

He finished his drink and pushed the glass in Bill's direction. If Bill wanted to hear the rest of the story it was going to cost him a drink.

"See, it was like this. We were hauling in our nets, keeping the ol' weather eye on some tough clouds building up to the south. Tweety said it would all blow past, but my uncle, see, he didn't see no point to taking no chances with a storm brewing and our holds full of fish. He wanted to make for port.

"That other captain must have seen them clouds, too, because he was sure piling on the coal to get up some speed. Boats like that are all right for a river or small lake, but they aint made for deep water and big waves. A smart captain knows it. So, she was heading to the nearest port to sit out the storm. That's how she ended up here in Saugatuck just before the murder."

"Murder?" Hack asked. "I never heard about some murder back then. You sure you got your facts right? Billy, you ever heard about such a thing?"

Bill shook his head. He had never heard about a murder.

"Sure, I got my facts right. It was kept real hush-hush." Old Chris laughed. "Tweety, he lit out of here for a couple of weeks when the police were nosing around. Now, buy me another bump and I'll tell you about it."

"That's just like you, telling some tall tale to get another drink," Hack said, but Bill waved him off and treated Chris to a third round, lit a cigarette, and leaned over the bar to hear the story.

The music wound down, and Thomas and Al packed up their guitars. "Get yourselves over here. You ever hear about a murder back in the '20s?" Bill asked. Thomas and Al shook their heads. They'd never heard of it, either.

Hack put his hand over Old Chris's glass. "Say, tell me something. First thing I want to know is if you survived this big storm you're telling about?"

Chris looked at him. "Well, yeah, you better believe I did. I'm sitting here next to you, aint I? Course I survived it."

"Just checking. And what became of that big storm that got you all scared and running for cover?" Bill asked.

"I figure it might have broken apart or just went on straight up north toward Holland or Port Sheldon or someplace. As I recall, we didn't get a lick of rain here in town, least not by the time we tied up at the dock."

"And you are absolutely, positively sure you did survive and didn't drown or something?" Hack asked.

"Ah, you're always messing with me. Now, pipe down if you want to learn something."

CHAPTER ONE

VENETIAN WEEKEND, 1928

"The Harbor Master says we can tie up here for the night, but I don't see any way to get your car off," Garwood explained to his boss.

"Well, that's all right. We're not staying that long. Just the night and then maybe we'll call it enough. I'm ready to head back south again in the morning. I won't need the car for one night. There doesn't seem to be much to this place, anyway. Tell Fred he's got the night off.

"What did you say was the name of this place?"

"Saugatuck. And before you ask, we're on the Kalamazoo River, so don't let nobody fool you into thinking that's Wisconsin on the other side," Gar answered.

"All right. We'll spend the night and turn around and go home in the morning."

"Back south? I thought you wanted to go up to Traverse City? It's only another day or so, and I hear tell it's mighty pretty," Garwood countered. It was just like the boss to want to go somewhere and then decide to come back early. The exception was if some work was involved, and then he was never in a hurry to quit and go home. "We can spend the night here and I'll give the engines and boiler the sharp eye once over, and we'll be in fine shape come morning. I'll give the old girl a clean bill of health and we can be on our way north, Doc."

"Well, we'll see, but don't count on it. I said I'm ready to go back home. Anyway, get the boat tied up and then I'm going to stretch my legs. And Gar, would you please tell your missus I'd like anything but beef? She's a good cook, but we've had it for three days running. That's sufficient. Maybe fish would be a nice change. I saw some shanties up the river, so there's got to be fish for sale somewhere."

"Yes, sir! And Doc, we went through a lot of coal. I'd be more comfortable if we took on some more in the morning before we head up north," Gar said, suggesting yet another time that they continue their vacation.

"Fish for dinner," his boss answered. "No beef!"

"Aye-aye. I'll have her do just that," he said. "We'll be tied up and get the gangplank lowered in two shakes of a lamb's tail, sir."

"No rush. My guess is that I can see everything from here. I doubt there will be anything that interests me. And Gar, any idea why they have that big barn right in the middle of town? Looks like an aero-drome. That doesn't make sense."

"Yes, sir. That's called the Big Pavilion. Dance hall, mainly, es-pecially this time of the year. All the big names come here to play. That's what brings folks here. See that sign over there? It's the Black-hawk Orchestra Band that's playing this weekend. Might be some pretty lively music, you know."

"I see." He had no idea who or what the captain was talking about. Music had long since lost its appeal to him. That especially applied to what he called 'modern stuff'. He detested it, and just about everything else connected with the modern world "Orchestra band?" he asked. "Gar, it's either an orchestra or a band. It can't be both. Never heard of such a thing. Neither has anyone else."

Gar ignored him, as he usually did when his employer was restless and prickly. Besides, he was busy supervising a couple of young fellows tying off the *Aurora*, bow and stern.

"You look like proper swell," Mrs. Garwood said admiringly as her employer was about to go down the gangplank. She used a whisk brush to remove a bit of lint from the right sleeve of his white suit, then adjusted his tie. She took pride in the way he looked, and considered it her self-appointed duty, responsibility, and privilege to always having him look his best. Always a good supply of fresh collars, starched shirts, ironed ties, his shoes polished, all put away in his cabin And a ramrod straight back. No slouching, even at his age. She admired that in a man.

"Run along and have a good look-see. Dinner will be at six. On the dot. Don't forget."

"As long as it is anything other than beef. Fish, Mrs. Garwood. Fish! I'll be on time," he answered.

"And you're never late, either," she smiled. For that, she was grateful. She looked a man who was punctual, especially if it was something tricky to cook like fish. Red meat could be a little forgiving; fish, never. She ran the sleeve of her blouse over the crown of his straw boater and handed it to him. She smiled. He was wearing it at a slight angle, almost a bit jaunty. That meant he was at least moderately cheerful. It's when he had his hat on straight that she worried.

That was one reason she liked these excursions on the *Aurora*. It got him out of town, away from work, and he lost some of the starch in his soul. At home he would never wear a sporty boater.

"It just turned three," she reminded him. "Dinner in three hours."

Straight, and still standing tall for a man his age, shoulders back, he walked at a good clip north down Water Street from the Crow Bar to the end, made the corner, and walked up Butler Street. He was a general on an inspection tour, his pale blue piercing eyes taking in everything. People, shops, more people. The town was crowded for the holiday weekend. Secretaries and shop girls had left Chicago early to come up to Saugatuck on the overnight packet ships. They came to relax in the sun, dance, walk along the beaches, and half of them eagerly anticipating moments of flirtation with some young men who might be husband material. And, if not husband material, a suitable diversion, and preferably a good dancer. There were young men, all of them dressed like dandies in double-breasted white seersucker jackets, open shirts, and straw boaters. These peacocks were on the prowl as well, looking for a young woman, but a future wife was probably not a high priority. And other peacocks more casually dressed, with rumpled white linen jackets and tennis shoes, the brim of their pork pie hat turned up in front. They sauntered and slouched their way down the street, hands in their pockets.

There were older couples, too, slowly meandering past the shops, stopping in front of each of them to look inside. Up from Chicago on the steamers, or from Detroit and Indianapolis, or even further away, on trains. They would flood into the boarding houses, sleepiin late, then snooze in hammocks and rockers on the porches, convincing each other they were having a grand old time.

The city was crowded, and it made walking a challenge. Long steps, short steps, pause, all the way down the sidewalks.

None of it impressed him, but then, neither was he in the mood for merry-making. Over the years he had all but forgotten how to relax enough to have fun. Truth be told, he was painfully lonely, and he knew it, even if he would never admit it out loud, much less to anyone else. And restless. He'd always been that way. In school, at medical school, at the hospital. But the past decade had been worse. Ever since Mae had passed away, and their youngest daughter two days later, both from the Spanish Influenza. Ever since his oldest daughter, Phoebe, had married his first assistant in surgery. He was skilled, and could have joined the practice, but he wanted to move on, be his own man, make a name for himself and moved – deserted him really – to start hanging out his shingle. Phoebe and the children, too, of course. The loneliness and isolation he had first felt as a young boy had grown and settled onto him and clung like church mold. The only thing he knew how to do was work, and when the loneliness surrounded him, to work all the harder. Anything else would be a sign of weakness. He used dignity and a sense of duty as a mask, a defensive wall, and over the years he had made that wall thicker and higher.

Taking a vacation was something he rarely did. He had to force himself, and even then, he tried to tie it in with a medical convention or visiting some of the major hospitals to see what other surgeons were doing. He could justify a break if it included something practical, and all the more so if he could travel on the *Aurora*. The motion of the water, and moving on the water comforted him.

He walked down Butler Street and came to a small park, a city square, complete with some benches under the lindens and elms. He found one that was empty and sat down. He scowled when he looked at his watch. A full twenty minutes had passed, and as far as he was concerned, he had seen everything Saugatuck could possibly have to offer. It was a mystery why so many people would come so far for what seemed like so little. Now, if there had been a nice restaurant with linen service, that would have made him happy. Or a book store. Saugatuck didn't look like a place where a book store could survive for long.

In an instant the loneliness crushed down on him. He watched several couples, walking either hand in hand or the woman holding her man's arm. He'd been like them – once. A long time ago. With Mae, when they were first courting and up to the end. That was before the war. Never since. A few times his brother or sister-in-law had made some introductions to eligible women, all of them worthy contenders, but he had recoiled. At first it was out of loyalty to Mae, even if she had been gone for a decade. Then, he recoiled out of revulsion and fear, protesting that it would interrupt his work and be a distraction. Even if he could fearlessly use a scalpel to cut into a living, breathing human being, intimacy terrified him.

He watched them, envious that they could be so carefree.

"Hey, mister, you want to buy some flowers?" a young girl called to him from the sidewalk. He looked her way and she walked over to him. She was about ten or so, maybe a little younger, well turned out in a simple dress, and had long blondish hair that was starting to curl. To his surprise, she smiled at him, and he smiled back. In one hand she was swinging a wicker basket with an assortment of fresh cut flowers. "They're only ten cents a bunch. Just one thin dime," she smiled again. "Bet your wife would like some nice posies."

He stood up and took off his boater. "Dime a bunch, huh? That seems like a fair price. How many do you have?"

She sat down on the bench next to him, and he instinctively shifted a few inches further from her, moving to the far end. The girl counted them. "I got ten left, mister."

"So, how much would it be to buy all of them?" he asked gently.

"Why, that would be a whole dollar!" she rolled her eyes in mock disgust that a grown man wouldn't know that ten bunches of flowers at a dime each would be a dollar. She didn't seem quick to want to make a package deal. "Do you want all of them."

"Yes. Yes, I think I do. I'll buy them all for a dollar, and then I'll give you another dollar if you deliver them for me. How does that sound?"

"That would be swell, mister!"

"Shake on the deal?" he smiled, holding out his hand. "What's your name, young lady? I always like to know who I'm doing business with."

"Phoebe. Pheoebe Walters. What's your....?" she started to ask She looked up at him she froze, terrified by the pain in his eyes and the way his face drained of color. "Are you okay?"

He recovered quickly. "Perfectly fine. You just caught me by surprise, that's all. I have a daughter with the same name – Phoebe Walters. Of course, she's much older and married and has children about your age. Your name just surprised me, that's all." He forced a smile at her again.

"Oh. I thought maybe I said something wrong or you were going to get sick all over me or something. Last year Scotty got sick all over teacher, but that was when we had a pop quiz in history," she said very seriously. Then she brightened up again. "And I like to know who I am doing business with, too. What's your name, mister?"

"Balfour. Doctor Horace Walter Balfour,"

"Well, I'm mighty pleased to meet you Doctor Horace Walter Balfour. And I appreciate your business." She held out her hand for the two dollars. "I'll take these to Mrs. Balfour. Which hotel are you at?" she asked.

"We came in by boat and tied up along the dock, just a little ways from the Crow Bar. She's called the *Aurora*, and you can't miss her.

If you take them there, ask for Mrs Garwood. She's my cook, and she'll know what to do with them. Oh, and you might ask her if she has some lemonade. I'll be she does. Just tell her that Dr. Horace said it was okay."

"Gee whiz! I sold all my flowers, I got a whole dollar to walk a couple of blocks, and lemonade. This is my lucky day!

"Mine, too. Now, run along and get those flowers into water, okay?"

Their conversation was interrupted when the town cop sauntered past. "Phoebe, you bothering this man?" he asked.

"Nope. This is my brand new friend Doctor Horace Walter Balfour, and he just bought all my flowers, and he paid me a whole dollar extra just to take them to his boat." She held up the two bills to show him. "How do you like that, huh, Callie?"

He was no longer interested in the young girl and turned to the man sitting on the bench. "I see. Horace Walter Balfour. Doctor Horace Walter Balfour. That name sure sounds familiar. Mine's Callahan, but everyone just calls me Callie," the officer said slowly, thinking it over, trying to remember where he had heard the name. "Say, you wouldn't be THE Doctor Balfour of the Balfour Hospital? Course you are. We'll, I'll be! Say, you thinking about hanging up your shingle here in Saugatuck. We'd draw a lot more people if they were coming to see you! A fellow like you would spiff up this place and bring in the business."

"Yes, I'm that Doctor Balfour, but I am here strictly on vacation, so I'd be grateful if you didn't spread it around." He stood up and looked the officer squarely in the face, his glare making his request into a command. "And no, I am not moving here."

"Say, I understand. But I got to tell you, the mayor is going to be some upset if he found out we had someone important here in town and he wasn't told about it." Callie said.

"That's unfortunate, but as I said, I am on vacation." His voice was calm and measured for a man not accustomed to someone disagreeing with him. The surgeon wasn't backing down.

"Sure is a shame he's over to Lansing at a meeting. He'll be real disappointed like to have missed you. He likes to meet folks like you.

"Say, bet you remember my cousin's boy, Roger? He had this leg that sort of locked up on him at the knee. I think he got it playing football, or maybe he fell out of a tree. Roger is his name. Roger Callahan. He must be around thirty by now, and lives down toward Glenn. If you saw him again I'll bet you would remember him. He sure would remember you. You probably did the operation on him. Say, I could take you out to his place if you wanted to say hello and look his leg over to be sure it's still working right," Callie offered.

Doctor Balfour turned away from him, rudely slighting him. He'd never cared for someone who thought too highly of themselves, and especially when they interrupted when he was talking with someone else. And that was al the more true if he was talking with someone younger than himself. "Miss Walters, thank you very much. I like the flowers and so will Mrs. Garwood. I'm sure they will be on our dinner table tonight. Now, don't forget what I said about the lemonade."

"Bye, Doctor Balfour. Don't worry. I'll remember!" She skipped down the sidewalk, her empty basket swinging from her right hand, toward the docks. No adult had ever called her "Miss Walters" before. It made her feel very grown up. She stopped skipping and walked. Grown-ups never skip, she told herself.

"Well, I must be going. Good day," Doctor Balfour said formally to the beat officer before he turned and walked through the park.

Doctor Balfour walked and wandered through the town for another hour or so, eventually returning to the *Aurora* long before dinner. To his surprise, Phoebe was still there. She and Mrs Garwood were sitting at a small table on the stern of the boat, a pitcher of lemonade between them, chatting as if they were old friends who had just run across each other after several years. "I thought I should wait to make sure you got home okay," she smiled at him. "You could of gotten lost, being a stranger here."

"Just a little girl talk," Mrs. Garwood hastily added. "Don't you worry. Dinner will be right on time as always." She got up to bring a glass for him, and he pulled up a chair. "Phoebe is pretty taken with your boat."

It made him smile. It was a good solid boat. Gar, and Royce down in the engine room, and sometimes some hired hands, kept it polished and painted. In port, Mrs. Garwood had no difficulty finding a couple of young women to do the cleaning, making sure everything was dusted and polished to perfection. A thorough job in the library and lounge, and everywhere else. The exceptions were her galley and Doctor Balfour's cabin. They were off limits to everyone but her.

"Do you know you can see the chain ferry from the back of your ship, Doctor Horace? It's right over there. Mother takes it every morning and evening. She should be coming any time."

"And what is a chain ferry?" he asked her.

"It's a ferry boat to get you across the river, but it's on a chain. Someone cranks it and it goes across the water. Come on, I'll show you. It's only a nickel round trip. I can afford it today. My treat. You too, Mrs. Garwood."

The older woman waved her off, saying that she had to get back to the galley.

"Come on, Doctor Horace. Mrs. Garwood tells me you've been practically everywhere in the world but you've never ridden on a chain ferry before. It's a lot of fun!" She held out her hand to take his, and practically dragged him down the gangplank and on to the side walk.

When they got to the shack of a deserted ticket booth Phoebe breathlessly explained. "So, this is the chain ferry, and you get on it just like a regular boat. You can stand or sit on a bench." She pulled a dime out of the pocket of her dress. "Two please," she told the young fellow who operated the boat. "If you ask real nice, sometimes he'll even let you turn the crank."

"That's quite the job," Doctor Balfour smiled at the ferryman. "You get paid for someone else doing the work. You should go into politics when you grow up, young man."

The young man ignored his comment. "All aboard!" the fellow shouted, then blew a whistle he had on a leather cord around his neck. Phoebe was surprised that the whistle made her new friend shudder. The young man began turning the crank, and slowly the ferry began crossing the Kalamazoo River. "See how it works? He turns the crank to pull us along."

"Ingenious," he murmured, enjoying the beauty of the river. It reminded him of the Root River back in Minnesota, where he had fished for trout as a boy. As always, when he was on the water, he became a different man.

"You sure you don't want to turn the crank?" she asked.

This time he didn't answer. His mind had gone back to his boyhood camping and trout-fishing days. Somewhere, probably up in the rafters of the carriage house, was the tube with his rods. He wondered if he still had the reel and flies. It had been so long ago, those afternoons of fishing...

She tugged urgently at his sleeve to recapture his attention. "Look, over there! That's mother!" Phoebe said loudly. She waved across the water to a woman standing next to her bicycle, waiting for her to return the gesture. "You'll get to meet Mother!" she said a second time. Even from a distance, Doctor Balfour could tell she was a stately looking woman. Certainly very attractive. She was perhaps in her thirties. His lips tightened when he saw her black hair, bob cut in the latest style. Either a well-to-do society woman who was pretending to be useful, or else a woman trying to convince herself and others that she was up to date. She wore khaki, loose-fitting trousers, a dark blouse, and had a handkerchief tied loosely around her neck. "Bright young things" as he had heard them called. Either way, he didn't like their type. His preference was to avoid them.

"She's a teacher at Ox-Bow. Bet you've never even heard of Ox-Bow, have you Doctor Horace?" When he told her he didn't know about the place, she added, "Then you've never been their either, have you? It's an art school. It's the most wonderful art school in the prettiest place I've ever seen in the entire world! You can paint and draw there and do all sorts of wonderful things. Mother teaches there, and when I grow up, I want to teach there, too!"

Doctor Balfour was ignoring her again, staring at the river as it made the last miles down the river and out to Lake Michigan. Water was always calming.

"Mother, this is my brand new best friend and customer, Doctor Horace Balfour, and he lives on the biggest ship I've ever seen and maybe the biggest ship that ever sailed into Saugatuck. And I got to sit on the deck in the back and wave at people as they went by, and drink lemonade, " Phoebe blurted out without pausing for breath. It was only then that she remembered to give her mother a hug, and the three of them got on the ferry to return across the river.

"It's a pleasure to meet you, Doctor," the woman said, extending her right hand. "I'm Harriet Walters, and I can tell you've already met my daughter. I trust she wasn't imposing on your time or your hospitality." She turned to Phoebe and asked, "You did remember your Paris Manners, didn't you?"

Phoebe rolled her eyes. "Yes, Mother." She was, after all, completely and totally grown up, and didn't need to be treated like a child. Or, so she thought.

"May I help you get your bicycle on board, Mrs. Walters," Doctor Balfour asked.

"Thank you. No. I am perfectly capable of managing on my own," she said with a twinge of glacial firmness in her voice. He felt no need to reply, and they rode the ferry back to the other side in silence. Instinctively he pulled his shoulders back and stood straighter. A rude Bright Young Thing, he thought. She brought out the starchiness in him.

"Well, it's been a pleasure to meet you both. Phoebe, thank you for having such beautiful flowers to sell. They are going to look very nice this evening." He gravely shook hands with her, then turned to her mother. "Mrs. Walters, a pleasure." He touched the brim of his boater.

"Oh, but we're coming to dinner with you," Phoebe said brightly. "Mrs Garwood said you always like to have guests, so she invited us!"

"Phoebe!" her mother snapped hotly. "You are an impossible girl. Absolutely not! We're going to have a talk about manners and good behavior the moment we get home. And then it is straight to your room so you can think about how a young lady deports herself!"

Doctor Balfour was taken by surprise, but he recovered instantly. Yes, he sometimes had guests at his table, but they were either family members or visiting physicians, and never someone he just met and barely knew. He surprised himself and came to Phoebe's rescue. "Well, this is awkward, but your daughter is quite right. I do enjoy having guests for dinner, and I am very happy that Mrs Garwood picked you two to be our guests for this evening. I eat alone enough as it is, and you two are the only people I've met here. Wonderful! Please join me, unless you have other plans."

"Please, Mother?" Phoebe begged.

"Indeed, please do say yes, Mrs. Walters," Doctor Balfour echoed. "I suspect by now Mrs. Garwood is planning on guests."

"We don't have anything planned for tonight, Mother. Please, can we? Can we go? Please? It's a wonderful ship, and we can eat on the deck and wave at people going by."

"All right. But you and I are still going to have a long talk about behavior, young lady. I'm mortified the way you can impose yourself on people," she said.

"Capital!" He clapped his hands. "Phoebe, I don't suppose you know what we're having for dinner do you?" Doctor Balfour asked.

"Mrs. Garwood said I could choose whether we were having fish or beef. I said beef because we always have a lot of fish, and besides, she already had it on hand so there was no point in wasting it. And vegetables. And she said that by now you have probably found at least one place that sells ice crème because that is your favorite dessert. Vanilla ice crème with thick fudge sauce, extra helping. Am I right?"

"Beef, huh? Well, that's a surprise!" he said, trying to sound enthusiastic. "You're absolutely right about the ice creme, young lady, so a double scoop for you! That is, if it is all right with your mother." He looked at her for some sign of approval. Her lips were tight in disapproval.

"I always like guests. When we're on the *Aurora* we're quite informal and we all share at least one meal a day. You'll have a chance to meet Mr. and Mrs. Garwood, Fred who drives for me, and Royce the stoker. Good people, all of them," Doctor Balfour said.

Doctor Balfour began to relax during dinner. The young girl had somehow warmed his heart and broken through a small chink in the wall he had built around himself. He liked her. He genuinely liked her, and that was more than could be said about almost all other children. Even if own grandchildren were serious and cautious around him. So were most adults, and he returned the favour. Above all, she made him laugh. Her mother was another matter. Harriet Walters didn't relax. Throughout the entire meal she sat without once slouching or relaxing against the back of the chair. She was unwaveringly tense, and almost excruciatingly polite and formal.

When the Garwoods were cleaning off the dishes, Mrs. Garwood stopped her husband in the galley for a moment. "She's more tightly coiled than the boss." He just smiled, wondering which of them would defrost the first, or last the longest.

As she took out the last of the plates, Mrs. Garwood turned around to ask, "Why don't I send Gar in to town to get us a pail of ice crème, and you folks just sit here and enjoy the evening while I finish tidying up?"

"I'm quite sure we have already over-stayed our welcome," Mrs Walters said. "We really must be on our way home."

"Phoebe, if I'm correct, I'm sure that Gar or I promised ice crème," Doctor Balfour suggested. She nodded. Then, turning to her mother he said, "I'd hate for your daughter to think I'm not a man of my word."

"If you insist," she said. "And, it is rather nice being on your boat."

"And we can't forget the fudge sauce. Gar, if you're getting some, make sure you get enough!" their host said.

"Aye aye, Sir," Gar said, touching the top right side of his forehead. "I'll get double the usual!"

"Mother! Why don't I go with Gar into town and show him where the ice crème store is? It'll save time. And you and Doctor Balfour can sit here and watch people. We wouldn't be all that long. Please," Phoebe suggested.

"That's very kind of you, young lady, but you see Gar is a boat captain, and it is a well known fact that all captains have an incredible sense of direction. Their nose always points due north. Just watch and see. He'll be back in no time," the doctor replied quickly, seeing right through her scheme to let the adults talk and get to know each other.

An hour later, as mother and daughter were walking home from the *Aurora*, Mrs Garwood stood next to her employer as they looked down at the street from the deck. "I'd say she has her cap set for you." Doctor Balfour ignored her, watching until they turned the corner and disappeared from sight. Mrs Garwood repeated her comment, this time a bit louder.

"Don't be ridiculous," he snapped, stiffening. "Not everything is what it first appears. Only a first- year medical student makes a snap diagnosis. You'll do well to remember that."

"We'll see," she teased. "No woman is that cold unless she's interested in a man and playing hard to get. She has her cap set for you, you'll see. Mark my words. I'm just saying."

His eyes lit up in anger. "That is a topic that will not be discussed again, is that clear?" The storm was over. He calmed down and changed the subject. "When I was in town this afternoon I bought a couple of tickets for you and Gar to that Blackhawk Band over at that big barn. It's been a while since you had an evening out, so, as long as we're here.... Oh, and one for Fred and one for Royce. Keep an eye on Royce. He's a bit young to be left to his own devices. I don't want him getting into trouble." He pulled the four tickets out of his jacket pocket and handed them to her. "I think if you hurry you won't miss too much of it. And remind Gar we're leaving in the morning."

"What about you? Don't you want to come along, too?" she asked.

"No, it's an evening out for the four of you. My treat. A evening out for all of you."

She thanked him for the tickets. She knew there was something strange about him. He could have ice for blood one moment, and then turn around and be incredibly thoughtful the next.

"What do you suppose Himself will do tonight?" Gar asked his wife, holding her hand to guide her through the crowds on the street, all of them migrating toward the big wooden building.

"Same as always. Turn off most of the lights and go to the library to read for a while. And then go down to his cabin like he does every night. Poor man. He's lonely as anything and can't help himself. Or doesn't want to." She didn't add that Doctor Balfour would take the small picture of his late wife out from the bureau drawer and put it on the nightstand next to his bed. First thing in the morning he would return it to the drawer and put it under his shirts. On the *Aurora* she was both cook and housekeeper, and knew the importance of being discreet. Gar didn't need to know all the secrets.

If he thought he was hiding his pain from Mrs Garwood, he was wrong.

CHAPTER TWO

Garwood waited until after his employer had his breakfast and a second cup of coffee before he gave him the bad news. "Doctor Balfour, I hate to tell you this on account of the fact it'll make you sore, but we're not going anywhere until we take on some more coal," he began softly. "We burned through a lot of it yesterday outrunning that storm. We don't have enough to get much past the breakwater."

His boss grimaced. "I see. You mentioned something about that yesterday. I trust there is coal here in Saugatuck?" he asked.

"That there is. And we're lucky for that or we'd have to have it trucked in. The problem right now is getting to it. The North America is ahead of us and got things bottled up for at least s couple of hours. I talked to the harbour master, young fellow named Peterson, and he said he can get us loaded up once she's out of the way. He'll have a tug get us up to the collier."

"I see," Doctor Balfour said. He detested vacations. He detested waiting even more. "So, we're looking at being stuck in the waiting room until this afternoon at the earliest?"

"Yeah, but that won't do us much good. We'll get out on the lake and only have a few hours of daylight. Now, we could make it to Holland for sure, maybe to Grand Haven, but only if we're lucky and we get the wind to our back."

"That's north. I told you last night I'm ready to go home. I've changed my mind about going to Traverse City. We're heading back south."

"That being the case, we could make it to South Haven by dark, but no further. And, we'll have the wind against us the whole way."

"Fine. Be that as it is, then. It can't be helped. All right, we're sitting in the waiting room for a few hours this morning." Doctor Balfour slammed his fist against the teak railing. It was about as much emotion and anger as he ever expressed, and he usually saved it for when he was alone after a patient had died during surgery.

Gar stood his ground, knowing that his boss would calm down as quickly as he flared up.

"Okay, Gar, I'll leave this in your hands. I might as well take some exercise and go for a walk. We'll cast off the moment we get the coal, even if it means delaying lunch!"

"We'll do our best. Say, maybe you'll run into that nice lady again. She's a looker, and that's for sure. Just don't go telling the missus I said that."

"I hope not!" Doctor Balfour snapped. A few hours with her last night had been more than enough to last him a lifetime.

Gar wisely dropped the subject. "Well, we'll be gone as soon as we can. South Haven tonight, and then if the wind isn't too much against us, we should make it into Chicago late tomorrow," Gar said as his employer stormed down the gangplank. "I'll tell you what, if we get a move on and can leave early I'll blow the whistle three times and pause and then three more times. That'll be the signal. Three blasts, pause, three more. Soon as you get aboard we'll cast off," the captain shouted down to the sidewalk.

It took him two blocks of stalking down Water Street before he cooled down. Mrs Garwood walked over to where her husband was standing, just in time to see Doctor Balfour before he turned a corner. "His hat's on straight," she sighed. The boss was in a foul mood.

He followed the same route from the day before, turning down Butler Street, eventually finding a shop that had newspapers for sale. A day old, brought in by a steamer the night before. He bought several and then walked back to a nearby park to find a bench as far away from the sidewalk as possible. He was in no mood for company, and knew he could safely hide from the world behind the broadsheets.

"Hello, Doctor Balfour!"

He recognized the voice and pulled down his paper. "Well, this is a delight, Phoebe. No flowers for sale today?"

She giggled and answered. "I sold them all!" and held up two crisp new dollar bills as proof.

"I see. Now, let me hazard a guess. You went for a walk down by the docks thinking you'd see me, and when I wasn't there Mrs Garwood bought your poesies and told you that you'd probably find me on a park bench reading the morning papers. Am I right, young lady?" he asked.

"Gosh! That's swell. You're a regular detective!" she gushed, her eyes wide open.

"Well, not really, except when it comes to medicine. So, tell me, what are you going to do today now that you're out of the flower business?"

"It's funny you should ask that," she said, suddenly becoming quite serious. "I really didn't have any ideas but Mrs Garwood said I should go into the tourist guide business. And that's what I'm doing. I'm your tour guide for the day."

"And how much are you charging as a tour guide?" he teased.

"Oh, it won't cost you anything at all. Captain Garwood gave me a whole dollar to take you around town for the morning. He said you could pay him back when we get back to your ship at noon. And, I'm staying for lunch because we're having beef stew. Oh, and we can't go too far in case he blows the whistle."

"No fish for lunch?" he asked.

"Nope, on account of the fact that there was left over beef from last night and Mrs Garwood and I agree, 'waste not want not' so it's stew."

"Well, it seems my day has been planned for me, hasn't it?" he asked. Surprisingly, he didn't seem to mind. If anything, Phoebe lifted his spirits. That surprised him.

"That's pretty much the way I see it, too! So come on. On your feet. There's lots to see." She held out her hand to pull him off the bench. To his surprise he didn't object to her holding his hand as she led him down Butler Street. They paused in front of each shop so she could tell him who owned the business, what they sold, and anything else that came to mind. She was a wealth of information, and seemed to know almost everyone who lived in Saugatuck.

At Hoffman Street they started up the hill. "Now, that's the Congregational Church," she said as they looked at a red brick building. "And that house," she said as they went another block, "that's where the richest man in the whole wide world once lived, but I can't remember his name. Anyway, he doesn't live there anymore. I don't know where he moved, but he doesn't live there anymore. Say, are you rich, Doctor Balfour? You must be to have a big ship like the *Aurora*. Bet you have a big home, too."

"Phoebe, it isn't money that makes a person rich. It's being happy. That, and having something useful to do is what counts the most."

She paused for a moment, looking up at him, thinking it over, and wondering why adults could never give a straight yes or no to a simple question. "I'm almost always happy. Sometimes Mother is happy, but not always. Are you happy?"

"Most of the time," he said softly. "I guess I never really think about it. Abe Lincoln once said a man is about as happy as he makes up his mind to be. Work makes me happy. And I'm happy right now because you are here." He had a feeling that the young girl was knocking a few chinks in that solid wall he had built around his heart. He knew he was letting her do it, too. Fortunately, he would soon be leaving Saugatuck before she made too big a breach.

They walked on in silence, holding hands, for another block.

"And there it is! That's the 'Piscopal Church! Isn't it pretty?"

"No, Phoebe, more than just pretty. It's beautiful. It reminds me of our church back home, except that ours is made out of brick. Wood is nice, too. What's the name of it?"

"All Saints! All Saints 'Piscopal Church! Mother says it was called because they started on All Saints' Day, but I think they called it that because we're all saints. So, I think it was named for us. What do you think?

"That's an interesting theological concept. It's almost too bad that you are a girl. You'd make a good minister thinking that way. What do you want to do when you grow up?"

"Oh, I want to become a veteran. Or maybe a teacher like Mother."

Doctor Balfour was confused. "A veteran? I think you mean veterinarian, don't you?"

"That's what I meant to say," she admitted softly. "Or a teacher. Mother says I should become a teacher because there are always jobs for teachers. Is that true, Doctor Balfour?"

"I think she's right. But remember, in a way, we're all teachers."

"I thought you were a doctor. Mother says that you are a world famous doctor, so how come you say you're a teacher?"

"Well, that's because I teach young men how to become doctors."

"Girls, too?" she demanded.

"Girls, too. Not many, but yes, a few." He was about to add that he had two women doctors working with him, but decided against it. Phoebe would only ask more questions.

She walked up the wooden steps to the door, then turned around and gave him a big smile. "Good! Mother says a lady should always be able to stand on her own two feet. Anyway, let's go in. You have to push on the door real hard. Put your shoulder up against it and push hard."

"We have to be quiet when we're in church," she whispered. "This is the bell tower, but you can't ring it except on Sunday mornings." She worked the latch on a very squeaky and clanky inner door.

"That would wake the dead," he whispered to her.

It took a few moments for their eyes to adjust to the low light coming in through the windows. Phoebe let out a little gasp of surprise. There was someone else in the church, sitting up in the front row, right in front of the pulpit. He suddenly stood up, a book in his hand, to greet them. "Good morning. I'm Reverend F. L. Smith. Welcome! You must be visitors. What a beautiful day to be out on a ramble."

"We're not visitors. Well, I'm not anyway. Mother and I are members here, but this is my friend and he's a visitor!" Phoebe explained. "This is my friend, Doctor Balfour." Both men reached out to shake hands.

"Horace Balfour," he said.

"Oh, my! Doctor Horace Balfour? THE Doctor Horace Balfour? Well, this is an honour. I can't wait to tell my wife that I shook hands with the most famous doctor in the world. Oh! Hope I didn't squeeze too hard. Can't damage a surgeon's hands, can we? Especially not yours! You saved a lot of good men in France back in '18. Not me fortunately! Well, I mean, I didn't NEED you to patch me up and save my life, that is. Mrs Smith will be disappointed she didn't get to meet you. Bet you're still saving lives. I reckon you are in the same business, just different departments. You do bodies; I do souls."

"Mrs Smith is a student at Ox-Bow," Phoebe explained, sliding in between the two men. "She's taking a painting class from my mother."

"Yes, you see, I'm just here for a week, filling in during the summer, while Mrs Smith is at the art school. We get a place to stay at the rectory next door in return for me doing services on Sunday, and she can study at the school."

"Interesting arrangement," Doctor Balfour observed. "Mutually beneficial all around. So, where did you go to school?"

Reverend Smith ignored the question. "Now, I can not claim to be anything of an expert on ecclesiastical art, but you will undoubtedly find the stained glass windows interesting. For example, let me show you the one above the altar. Just step this way, if you please, and you'll see the intensity of the colors from a different angle. Just relax your eyes, if you will, and you can see how the red and blue almost appear three dimensional. The red almost jumps out and the blue seems to recede. And yet, when you come up close, you'll see they are all the same thickness. That's Jesus as the Good Shepherd."

They looked at the windows for a good five seconds, and suddenly Reverend Smith began talking about something else. "Now, those lilies up in that little round window, well, ah, of course, they're an ancient Christian symbol."

Doctor Balfour looked closely at the increasingly strange, almost erratic minister. Even though the building was cool, he was perspiring.

"I don't think I'm feeling all that well, all of a sudden. If you'll excuse me, I'm going to step next door and lie down," the minister said. "Nothing serious."

"Yes, perhaps you should," Doctor Balfour said softly. He sniffed the air. No sign of strong drink. Perhaps the man was genuinely ill. Maybe he was nervous. Something was definitely wrong, but he couldn't figure out the cause.

Phoebe tugged on his coat sleeve. "We should be going, too," she whispered. "We've got to get back to your ship." He nodded in agreement, and watched as the strange man hurried out of the building.

"I thought you needed to be rescued," she smiled once they were outside.

"Very observant of you, young lady. And much appreciated.

They walked down the hill in silence until they came to Water Street. "You're a swell friend, Doctor Balfour. I wish you didn't have to leave so soon."

He didn't respond. He could hear the sound of the *Aurora's* whistle. It was time to leave. She walked with him back to his boat, and up the gangplank behind him.

"Thunderation! When you blew the whistle I took it to mean we were ready to leave. What do you mean we're going to be laid up for repairs? Gar, you said we needed to take on coal. Nothing about repairs. Why didn't you tell me earlier?" the old surgeon bellowed at the captain.

"That old engine's taken a beating over the years, and it didn't help none when we raced against the storm. Royce and me had the boiler at the redline most of the way here from the time we passed Pier Cover. We had to or we would have gone down, and that's for sure," Gar explained patiently. "Now, I've told you before those pipes are getting old, and you start putting that much pressure on old ones, especially like those, and you can have an explosion. Lot of those old steamers blew up on account of that, as you ought to know. This one was about to blow, too. Still is. That's why I've been telling you to switch over to oil, but you didn't want to do it, and now we've got a problem!"

Doctor Balfour continued to glare in hot fury. "Go on! Get to the point! What happened?"

"Real simple. Since we had to wait to get towed up for more coal, I fired her up to give her the close eye once over, and there was water coming out of the pump. She needs a new gasket. Otherwise, she's only going to get worser and worser once I get her up to full steam. That happens and if she don't get enough water into the works she'll blow. I had to steam down real quicky like. I opened the valves and we flooded the fire box and then I used the whistle to siphon off the rest of the steam. That's what you heard."

"So, we're dead in the water right now?" Doctor Balfour asked, beginning to understand just how serious the problem was, and how fortunate it was that Gar spotted the problem.

"That's about the size of things. But we sure would have been dead in the water if we'd headed out to the lake and the boiler blew. Dead corpses in the water is more like it, unless we went down with the ship. Dead. Mangled. Call it what you like, but it would have been a disaster and us in the middle of it. The ol' *Aurora* would have been blown to smithereens and kindling," Gar said.

"All right. I see. But you're the captain. What do we do to fix it?"

"I talked to that young fellow, Peterson, the harbour master I told you about, and he's got a master boiler man coming over quick as he can. He's up to the boat yard in Holland right now. Once she cools down in another hour or so and he gets back, then him and me'll have to take off the pump and strip her down. Then we cut a new gasket, put it in there and seal it up tight, and put the works back together. After that we'll fire up the boiler real gentle-like and hope she holds. If she does we ought to take her down to the mouth of the river and back a couple of times to make sure."

"And that means I'm still in the waiting room! Thunderation!" his temper flared up again.

"That's about the size of it. You, me, Mrs Garwood, Fred and Royce. We're all sitting in a real comfortable waiting room. And you might as well know that we gotta let that new gasket settle for a day. At least the chairs are more comfy than the ones at your office."

Doctor Balfour didn't find the last comment amusing.

"There is some good news," Gar continued, "outside of the fact that we didn't get blown up and killed dead. I got a tug coming down here to pull us around so Fred can get your car off."

"That's something in our favour, at least. Look Gar, thank you. You're a good man. You probably saved all our lives," Doctor Balfour said quietly. He was still angry, but he knew to control his temper.

By a sheer act of Providence, Phoebe was up on the deck, having a final goodbye lemonade with Mrs Garwood, waiting to say good bye to her friend. The older woman looked at Doctor Balfour as he came toward them and whispered to the girl, "Brace yourself. Storm clouds and heavy sailing, and that's for sure."

Doctor Balfour sat down hard on a chair and slumped down in defeat and frustration. He was not much of a slumper or sloucher except in the worst of times. Even when he was relaxing, he was ramrod straight. This time he slumped. He accepted a glass of lemonade and drank it quickly. "Well, young lady, looks like you got your wish. We're not leaving just yet, and that's for sure. Engine problems."

"That's all right. Mrs. Garwood told me about you not liking waiting rooms, so we'll find something fun to do. I'll keep you company so you won't be sitting by yourself. Maybe you and I can spend more time together. Or maybe you and Mr. and Mrs. Garwood can have dinner at our house tonight."

The old doctor said nothing. The girl frowned, wanting to do something to make him feel better.

"I'd like to see what's wrong. Maybe I could help," she offered.

"That's very kind of you, but really, there's really nothing you can do to help, even if you wanted to. And I don't think we should go down to the engine room just now," he said absently.

"So, could you draw what's wrong with the works?" she asked. "I'm sure Mrs Garwood must have a piece of paper and a pencil."

He smiled and nodded toward his cook. She returned with a pad of paper and some pens. Doctor Balfour began sketching out the water pump and showing her where the gasket was leaking. "This is the valve, and it's a good thing it's a machine. You have got valves in your heart, but if they start leaking there isn't much we doctors can do about it. Maybe someday, but not now. Gar can fix an engine better than a doctor can fix a heart. So, he'll take all of these bolts off, remove the gasket and cut a new one out of leather, put it in and seal it, and then fasten it all up again. Should be right as rain once he's done. When he is done, that is."

"I see," Phoebe said solemnly. She didn't have the slightest idea what her friend was talking about, but it seemed interesting, and certainly very important. She changed the subject. "You draw nice.

See, I knew there was something fun we can do while you're in the waiting room. We can go out to Ox-Bow and Mother could be your teacher! Instead of just drawing with a pencil you could paint with paints."

She didn't see his lips tighten in disdain. Fortunately, Phoebe didn't pursue the idea any further. Then, taking no chances, Doctor Balfour got up and went into his library and closed the door until it was time for lunch.

When it came to questions and curiosity, if anything, Phoebe was insatiable. She had just finished helping Mrs Garwood clear away the dishes when she returned to the table, sat down, and asked, "How did you decide to become a doctor?"

"Well, my father and his father, my grandfather, were both doctors, so I guess I just followed in his footsteps. Maybe that's what you're going to do: follow in your mother's footsteps if you become a teacher."

Phoebe thought about it for a moment and said solemnly, "I'll bet it is a lot of work becoming a doctor."

"Yes, you're right about that. More than anything else, it takes a lot of concentration. The best doctors are the ones who can make a good diagnosis first, and then they operate."

"Diagnosis? What's that?"

"Well, let's see. When a doctor has a patient in the examining room he does a thorough examination, head to toe, and sometimes we see or hear something out of the ordinary. And we ask a lot of questions. That's how we start figuring out what's wrong. Good doctors always, always, always do that. The not-so-good ones just listen to what a patient tells them and then jump in without thinking. We try to see or hear something that shouldn't be there. It's a start, anyway." He was trying to make years of medical training and decades of experience simple enough for her.

"I see," she said quietly, thoughtfully, remembering the few times her mother had taken her up to the hospital in Holland to see the doctors for a check up. "You mean like when Gar found the problem with the water pump and blew the whistle? That's seeing and hearing something wrong, isn't it?" she asked brightly.

"That's right. You see, most people will see something, but they don't have enough focus to really observe, and until they get enough experience, they can't really focus. Tell you what, I want you to look at the people as they walk past the boat, and see if you can figure out what they do for a living, or where they are from, or something else that makes them different from others. You don't have to get the city right – just whether they are from here or somewhere else for starters, and maybe why they came here. See if you can spot the difference between a shop keeper or a farmer or someone else." He pulled down his straw boater to shade his eyes, hoping that this would keep her busy, and quiet, for at least a few minutes."

For a few moments Phoebe concentrated as hard as she could on the street scene in front of her. "Okay, there's one. See that fellow in the white suit. The one with the face all pinched up like a rat. He doesn't seem to fit in at all. Nor the men who are with him, either," Phoebe said, pointing to a man in a bright yellow shirt and black tie, wearing a seersucker suit.

Doctor Balfour raised his hat just a bit and squinted in the direction where she was pointing. He was still too far away for him to make out the man's face. "No, no he sure doesn't. You've picked out one who doesn't fit in. Good girl. Now, what do you think he does for a living?"

They watched as he and two companions walked closer. "I don't know for sure. He looks sort of flashy, like he's a salesman or something. Maybe he sells cars. Or a musician, maybe."

The trio came closer. "Hey, the boat! Thought I recognized you in town earlier," the man shouted at them, smiling a toothy grin that was a partial sneer.

"We meet again," Doctor Balfour said without a smile.

"Say, you're a little far from home, Doc. Everything okay back there? No trouble or nothing, Horace? Not on the lamb are you?" He laughed. "You didn't have to get out of town in a hurry, did you?"

"Just fine," Doctor Balfour replied, tightening his lips.

"Say, you need a bottle or two, just let me know. I got some good stuff. Premium stuff, not that homemade poison. Canadian. First rate hooch. Just say the word, I'll be around. We're up here for a day or so."

"No thank you."

"It's good stuff. Comes from Canada. Premium," he repeated.

"I said no thank you," Doctor Balfour snapped.

"Your call. You change your mind, let me know. I'll be around. Complimentary, too." The man took off his boater and made a low bow, then went on his way having a laugh with his two friends. Doctor Balfour watched them saunter down Water Street, his face still tight with anger.

"He doesn't look like a very polite man," Phoebe said.

"You have no idea how right you are on that account," Doctor Balfour said flatly. He was silently seething at this chance encounter with the rat-faced man. He was the very sort of person he tried to avoid. "Vermin," he whispered out loud. "Rat-faced vermin." He glanced over at Phoebe, relieved that she hadn't heard him.

"I've seen him before here," Phoebe finally said. "I think he's from Chicago or someplace really big. You can tell from the way he's dressed he's a real swell."

"You see to it you keep your distance from him and people like him. That's all I'm saying. Now, forget about him. See if you can spot someone different."

The girl soon returned to her people-watching, and Doctor Balfour once again pulled his hat down to shade his eyes. "Now, there's someone much more interesting! They look like nice people," she said brightly, pointing at two men and a woman, about half a block away. Her elderly friend ignored her prattle.

"See, they look different," she told him, tugging on his sleeve to get his attention. The second time he looked up and turned in their direction. A smile burst across his face. "Well, of all the people...."

In a flash he was on his feet and out of his chair, striding across the deck in long steps and hurrying down the gangplank to the street. It was the first time she had seen him smile and so active all day. It surprised her that he could move so fast. Phoebe didn't know if she should stay where she was or follow behind him. She decided to remain in her chair and watch from the deck.

One of the two men shouted, "Horace!"

"Theo! Clarice! What in the world are you two doing here?" he asked.

"More's the question, Horace, what are you doing here? Don't tell me that you are taking a real vacation, just sitting on your boat and taking in the sun? You feeling alright? Need to see a doctor or something?"

The old doctor tipped his head back and laughed. "I'm fine, perfectly fine, except I'm not here by choice. It's a long story, but we had to outrun a storm and ended up here in Saugatuck. And now we've got engine problems. The water pump has a bad gasket and Gar says it's about to burst. He's working on it, but that means I'm sitting in the waiting room."

"Not the worst waiting room in the world. I told you before you ought to get rid of that old scow," Theo replied. "You ought to get one of those cigarette boats that came out. Something fast and sleek." He was teasing, knowing full well that his brother would never do it.

"Now, what are you two doing here? Come and join me on the deck."

"First of all, there are three of us, just in case you didn't notice. Clarice you already know, of course. This is Doctor Mason. I don't know if you two have met. We were at a surgeon's meeting in Chicago and had dinner, and he said he had a cottage up here and invited us to come along for a day or so. I didn't think we'd find you here." His brother Theo explained.

"Not much of a cottage, more like a cabin, but it's my home away from home. Mrs Mason said it's more like a broken down shack," the second man explained. "I'm Mason, by the way." He stretched out his right hand.

Theo interrupted to tell more of his story. "Anyway, it's at this place called Ox-Bow. Some sort of art colony or something. You won't like it. Trust me. Too Bohemian for your tastes. And just to put the frosting on the cake, Mason here said that the Blackhawk Orchestra is playing at the Big Pavilion. Knowing you, you've never heard of it. Well, they're here, and I happen to know the fellow who plays brass. An old buddy from the war. Never mind, you're already falling behind. Anyway, you're about the last person I expected to find among the Bohemians and locust eaters."

"Never mind all that. Like I said, it's not by choice. Anyway, come on up and have something cold to drink." The three of them followed him up the gangplank. "And this is my city guide and self-appointed general right hand-man and first assistant, Phoebe Walters," the doctor said, making introductions.

"Right-hand girl, Doctor Balfour. I'm a girl, not a man," she said, rolling her eyes.

"And a feisty one, too," Doctor Mason said. "How's tricks, Phoebs? You still doing what your mother tells you and behaving yourself? What does she call it – 'Paris Manners' or something?" he smiled, giving her a hug. "Phoebs and I are old friends," he explained to his friends.

"And Phoebe, this is my younger brother, Doctor Theodore Balfour. Theo for short, and his wife, Mrs. Balfour," he continued.

"You mean I've got two Doctor Balfours to take care of?" She rolled her eyes in mock disgust. "Are you sure you're really and truly brothers? You don't look at all like each other," she sighed.

"We've been studying the importance of observation," Doctor Balfour explained.

"Yes, Phoebe, that will be a problem. It's always been a problem, and would you believe it was even worse when their father was still alive? Then there were three of them. So, back home everyone just called them 'The Old Doctor' for their father, and Doctor Horace and Doctor Theo. We could do that here so it won't be so confusing," Mrs. Theo Balfour suggested.

"Mother would say it's terribly informal," Phoebe said solemnly. Then she brightened up, "Okay, by me!"

"Horace, you wouldn't happen to have anything on board that's a tad stronger than lemonade, would you?" Theo asked.

"Too bad you weren't here a few minutes ago. Our old friend Frank just offered to sell me something," Horace said, trying to force a smile.

"Frank? You mean I think you mean?"

"The one and same. Frank Nitti," Doctor Horace answered. He shook his head in disgust.

"We get all types up here during the season," Doctor Mason explained. "You'd be amazed at who all comes here. Big name musicians and bands. Writers, artists, bankers. They draw in the good, the bad, and the riff-raff. Frank Nitti isn't the worst of them. His boss comes up here, too. Bond salesmen and bankers; they're even worse. They're the scary ones. Makes it interesting around here in the summer."

"Nitti's boss comes up here?" Doctor Horace asked.

"Most the time he's down to South Haven playing golf, but he comes up here once in a while to have a little fun. No one says anything about it. What surprises me is that you two know Frank and Snarky...."

"My brother and I had a shotgun wedding with them. We provide the medical care and they make sure there's no crime back home," Theo explained.

"It's a pact with the devil!" Horace said hotly. His younger brother ignored him.

"Working out?" Doctor Mason asked.

"Let's just say that we get more than our share of lead poisoning and ah, certain diseases, but the streets stay safe and quiet," Theo answered. "No one's robbed the bank, at least."

"About the best I can offer you is lemonade," Horace said firmly. Doctor Mason could sense the tension between the two brothers. It was obviously a sore subject between them, based on expediency. He was eager to change the topic.

"Say, it's hotter than blazes in town. Tell you what, there's always a cool breeze over to Ox-Bow. Why don't we drive over and I'll show you around. And show off my new cottage. You might even want to think about taking up painting as a hobby. You ought to at least give it a try. Relaxing. Might do you some good," Doctor Mason said.

"That's the exact same thing I told him," Phoebe added.

He turned to the young girl. "Phoebs, you coming with us or do you want to stay here? That is, if it is all okay with Doctor Horace."

"Of course it is," Horace answered. "Gar and his wife can look after her, or she can come with us. Phoebe, it's your decision."

She screwed up her face in concentration as she weighed her choices. "I'll stay here, thank you. I can go to Ox-Bow any time, but I can't always wave at people from a ship!"

Doctor Theo and his wife both laughed. "That's a highly intelligent woman you hired as your assistant. Couple of years from now we could use a new secretary or two like her. She might be a good one if she can keep you in line," Theo said.

"I believe Miss Walters has plans on becoming a doctor. Better watch yourself Theo or she might be replacing you," Horace told him.

"All right you two. Enough of this sibling rivalry. Tell you what, Phoebs. I parked up by the Episcopal Church. I'll go up and bring it down here. If you change your mind in the meantime, you're welcome to come along with us. That Jake with you?" Doctor Mason asked.

To Doctor Horace's shock, Phoebe spit in the palm of her right hand, hit it with her left first and answered, "Jake with me!"

"I'll bet your mother didn't teach you that!" Horace teased. "That would never pass for Paris Manners, would it?"

"Nope, it sure wouldn't, and I don't care. But you don't need to tell her, please," she bantered back. Everyone laughed, and that made her happy.

Doctor Mason pulled up in a black Dodge touring car, tooted the horn, and waited for the three Balfours to get in. Phoebe hadn't changed her mind. She was leaning on the rail of the *Aurora* to wave them on their way. "The drive isn't all that long. It's probably just as short to take the chain ferry over, but climbing up that hill in this heat is a bear in this weather. This'll be easier," Doctor Mason said as he inched his way past pedestrians and other cars.

"Oh, and I was so looking forward to cranking the chain ferry," Horace said with a tickle in his voice.

"You, cranking a chain ferry, Horace?" Doctor Mason asked. "Now, I could see Theo doing that, but I always heard you were a bit too stiff and formal to engage in that sort of raucous behavior. I would have thought it was beneath your dignity. Saugatuck can work wonders on some people!"

Once they got out of town they picked up speed, crossed the Kalamazoo River and turned right to follow the road a few blocks, and then right again onto a road that ran parallel to the river. On both sides were cottages, some rather expensive, some little more than shacks. "Brick building over to the right is the pumping station," Doctor Mason said. "Hold on to your hats."

He blew three long blasts on his horn, waited a good ten seconds, blew the horn again, then shifted down to first gear and raced up the final dune on a narrow one-car dirty trail. "Made it!" he said as they stopped on a sand and gravel parking lot. "Welcome to Ox-Bow, home of fresh air, no electricity, no citified amenities, outdoor privies, and the smell of oil paint. Pretty, huh?

He continued his spiel before anyone could answer. "Over there's the Old Inn. I understand it used to be a hotel back in the day when the river came through here. Someone told me that President Roosevelt spent the night here once, and the great James Fenimore Cooper himself wrote some of his novels here. Maybe, maybe not, but that's what folks like to say. Bet some of them believe it, too. Pretty place, though. It's the art school now.

"Over there, along the river, those are more painting studios. And up there a few of us have got our own places up in the dunes in the woods. You know Tallmadge the architect? He's got a place here. Let's stretch our legs and have a look-see, and then I'll show you my place."

Doctor Horace felt himself stiffening up, and it had nothing to do with the bumpy ride or tight back seat of the Dodge. It was the informality of the place, and the strange surroundings. He was never good with the unfamiliar. A new restaurant was a trial for him, and this somewhat shabby looking art camp was well beyond that. It brought out the worst of his pomposity. "I thought you arty types wore smocks and berets," he said icily.

"Well, they only do that in Paris, but that's mainly for the benefit of the Americans. They figure they have to look like artists to sell anything. You remember that painter out on the street, Theo? The one you bought those paintings from? He looked the part. Here, it's a bit different. No one has to pretend, so they just take things casual and easy out here," Doctor Mason explained.

"Trust me, Horace, you'll survive," Clarice said softly to him, put her hand on his arm. "There, there. I'll protect you."

He growled back at her.

They walked across the stiff grass of the meadow toward the lagoon, sending up swarms of gnats and mosquitoes. "Beautiful, isn't it? No place in the world compares to right here. See those posts sticking up from the water? That's where the old wharf was years ago, back before they cut a new channel out to the lake. Beautiful, just beautiful," Doctor Mason said softly. He swept his right arm out to display the view.

To his surprise, Horace saw a woman model posing on the deck, a group of young painters at their easels surrounded her. His eyes widened in alarm. "That woman's stark naked!" he objected.

"Horace, we've seen naked bodies before. We're doctors, remember?" Theo teased.

"Of course. But not out in public!" he objected. "That's scandalous!"

"All part of the beauty of nature, Horace. You know, you could be a model. Or better, if Theo says its alright, perhaps I'll pose," Clarice teased. She felt his entire body stiffen and tense up. He was relentless and eager to leave. "Perhaps they'd hire you as a male figure model," she repeated. Horace said nothing, as he straightened his boater and looked in another direction.

"Well, if we go up this way you'll get a chance to see my cottage. Now, fair warning – it's not much. Just a shack really. Place to stay and paint, and sleep," Doctor Mason said, leading them toward the woods.

The word 'shack' was optimistic. White painted clapboard, a few windows, and a small porch accessorized by a straight back wooden chair and an easel. A padlock secured the front door. "You come up here in the winter, too?" Horace asked.

"Not a chance. No way to get up that hill when there's snow. Not in a car anyway and I don't plan on using snow shoes. I didn't bother to insulate it, even. Strictly a warm weather place" He unlocked the door to show off a single room with a bed along one wall, a table and a couple of chairs. The air inside was stale and musty. "Rustic as they come. No electricity, no water. Ah, wilderness! Like I said, the privy's down the path. For some reason I can't get Mrs. Mason to come out here very often."

"I can't imagine why," Doctor Horace muttered.

"Well, I think it's charming," Clarice said bravely. "Not my sort of home, but you do like it, don't you, so isn't that all that really matters."

"Nice little hunting lodge or fishing camp," Theo said. Clarice looked warily at him, knowing that he envied his friend having a hideaway of his own. She could see him thinking, and wasn't enthusiastic about it.

Horace thought the whole thing could be improved with a little coal oil and some matches, but he kept his thoughts to himself.

"Say, long as we're here, let's leg it up to the Crow's Nest!" Doctor Mason said cheerfully. "Great view of the trees from up there. You need to get the full experience to really appreciate this place."

"You folks go ahead. I think I'll go back down to that main building. There's a swing on the porch that looks awfully inviting, provided it doesn't collapse and fall down," Horace said. "You three go on and have your fun. I'll meet you back there."

Doctor Horace relaxed on the swing, positioning a pillow behind his back, then twisting and turning so he could look across the meadow toward the lagoon, without having to watch the artists and their model on one of the docks. Here and there were small groups of students, some of them perched on camp stools at their easels, others sitting Indian-style on the grass with their sketch pads. All of them seemed quite content and focused on their work. It struck him that it was a different type of focus and intensity from what he had seen of medical students in laboratories. These young people were openly enjoying themselves, having fun.

Art and music had never held much appeal to him. His life was medicine, science, and the operating room. Much of the rest of his waking hours was spent with the administrative side of his practice. After that, when he got home in the evening, he relaxed by working on an article for one of the medical journals. Even without a family, there wasn't much time left for anything else. It wasn't that he was opposed to art; he'd just never given it much thought, and it almost always caught him by surprise that anyone would take seriously a career as an artist.

From time to time a young man or woman, sometimes an older one, a teacher perhaps, would come in through the screen door to the porch and pass him. A few of them murmured a quiet 'hello'. Most of them ignored him. One energetic young man greeted him with a boisterous "Hiya, Pops!" before going into a lounge-like gallery, leaving the aroma of beer trailing behind him. Doctor Horace got off the swing a few minutes later and wandered into the main building, making his way into the lounge.

Some of the paintings on the walls were quite nice. Pastorals. Mainly different paintings of the lagoon or the woods. They had a certain charm and a unique style. Trunks of trees, some lower branches, a low horizon line, and the top of the trees seemingly cut off at the top. And always water. A few were decidedly strange, hideously modern. His lips tightened as he tried to make sense of them, turning his head from one side to the other, wondering if perhaps one of them had been hung upside down.

"Like anything you see?" a woman's voice asked from the doorway. Doctor Horace turned around. It was Phoebe's mother, Harriet.

He touched the brim of his boater, then gave her a thin smile before saying anything. "Good afternoon, Mrs. Walters," he said. Remembering he was inside and in the presence of a lady, he took off his hat. "A couple of them are very well done. I was just thinking they might look rather nice in a waiting room in the hospital. Perhaps a patient's room. Rather calming and comfortable."

"They're all for sale," she said. "That one that you're looking at is twenty-five dollars."

"That's ridiculous," he retorted.

She flared up and snapped, "I'll have you know the artist spent a lot of time working on that painting. It's very well done. Surely you wouldn't begrudge an artist a decent price! Never mind the artist isn't internationally known and acclaimed – yet!"

"Absolutely not. Of course not. But twenty-five dollars is practically giving it away. It's underpriced. Whoever painted it deserves more than that. But then I've never known an artist or musician with a head for business. That's usually their problem. They're their own worst enemy when it comes to being practical."

Harriet's mouth tightened. "I see. And just what do you think is a fair price, Doctor Balfour?"

"At least a hundred. If you want my opinion, and you probably don't, any artist who sells a painting for twenty-five dollars is always going to stay a twenty-five dollar artist, and they can forget international acclaim. That painting is worth at least a hundred. I'd go even higher if the painter had the common sense and sufficient self-confidence to ask for it. It isn't even signed, so it tells me the painter thinks so little of his skill that he'll never go far."

"I see!" She spat out the words in a hurry, turned, and stormed out of the building, intentionally slamming the screen door behind her. He watched as she quick-marched across the meadow down to a small fishing shack and dock at the edge of the woods. She kept her back to him, refusing to allow him to see her cry.

Doctor Horace stared at her for a few minutes, perplexed as to what could have set her off. He'd only said something that made common sense. He debated whether to go after her, but then he spotted Doctor Mason leading Theo and Clarice back from their hike. They paused for a moment, and Clarice left the two men and quickly walked over to join Mrs. Walters.

"I'm sorry to say this, but your husband is a horrid man," Harriet sniffled.

"Oh, not my husband. Mine's the nice one. It's my brother-in-law who can be absolutely horrible at times, as I think you have discovered by now, she said gently. "Most of the time, some days. Well, truth be told, most days most of the time."

"I'm sorry. No, I'm not sorry for saying it. Well, I am, really. I mean, it's none of my business. And I'm sorry for you having to put up with him in your family. Oh, I'm not making any sense at all," she blubbered, accepting a handkerchief from Clarice.

"You're making perfectly good sense. I understand exactly what you're trying to say. Now, the first thing is to breathe and blow your nose, and then please listen. Horace isn't horrible at all. He's abrupt, short tempered, formal and icy, and the second best surgeon in the country. Right after my husband. For what it's worth, I think he's scared of anything that is unfamiliar to him. That's why he hides behind his work. Well, that and trying to live up to his standards of being a patrician. He wasn't always that way. It's been his nature for the last ten years, but that's another story. Now, he's stuck in a rut that way. It's me who is sorry that he upset you," she gently purred to calm her.

"Is he always like that?" Harriet asked.

"My dear, sometimes when we're back home I think my main job in life is to smooth over the feathers Horace has ruffled. Sometimes it's with Theo, sometimes with his daughter, usually with someone else." She held up her right hand, moving her fingers. "Let's see. Family, friends, other physicians, politicians, businessmen, people he's known for years. Everyone has experienced frostbite from him. I've spent years calming the waters. Now, just what did he say?"

Harriet didn't say anything at first. "It seems silly now, but I had a painting in the gallery for sale for twenty-five dollars and he said it's worth a lot more and that I didn't have any business sense. He said I'd be a fool not to take a hundred dollars. Well, not in exactly those words, but that's the general idea."

"Mrs. Walters...."

"Please, call me Harriet," she said.

"Very well, Harriet, it is. First of all, does Horace know that you painted the picture?"

"I don't know. We didn't get that far. No, probably not. He pointed out it wasn't signed."

"And do you want to sell the painting?"

"Well yes, of course!"

"Good. And a hundred dollars is much better than twenty-five, don't you think?"

"I'm not a child. Of course it is!" Her voice was defensive.

"Then I think you should get everything you can for it. You see, when Theo came back after the war he had bought some paintings off some French artist he met. The man did some good work but he was new to it and he couldn't get much. Theo bought five paintings fot a hundred dollars, cash money, right off the street. I thought they were the most God-awful things the cat drug home. Horrible. I told Theo I wouldn't have them in my house, and that he could put them in the garage or hang them up in his office if they wouldn't scare the patients. Well, they're worth a fortune now, and they are still as ugly as sin. But there's a lesson here – get everything you can for a painting, because if they're any good, someone will get more for them later."

"Who was the artist?" Harriet asked. "Do you remember?"

"Oh, some fellow named Dufy. Raoul Dufy," Clarice said casually.

"Your husband bought Dufy's paintings for twenty dollars a piece?" Her mouth dropped open.

"Now, when you've composed yourself, I suggest we go sell a painting. Come along, dear, and stay out of my way. Let me do the talking. I know how to handle the great Doctor Horace W Balfour! Watch as I put him in his place." The two women set off across the meadow, arm in arm, for the Old Inn. By the time they got to the screen door, Harriet was laughing. Clarice had triumphed again.

"Horace, you are absolutely right. Those paintings are undervalued. The one you are looking at and the other one next to it. Now, I've had an interesting conversation with Mrs. Walters. I think she's an up and coming artist. You remember when Theo came home with those paintings by Dufy? I think she is just as good and has just as much potential. At least you can tell what they are.

"What's more, I agree with you. I think they're undervalued at a hundred dollars. Mrs. Walters has said she'll take nothing less than a hundred and a quarter for each of them. EACH! Two paintings by an up and coming artist for two-fifty. Consider it an investment." She held out her hand, waiting for the money. From the corner of her eye Clarice could see Harriet swallow hard as if she had witnessed the great Houdini pull off his finest magical trick. She resisted the urge to let her jaw drop.

The two women watched as he reached into his jacket pocket for his wallet.

"Say, Horace, as long as you're collecting art, there are some other pieces you might want to see," Doctor Mason said. "On that wall over there are a couple of small pieces by a woman out of Illinois, Sylvia Mueller. And right next to her are a couple of small paintings by Cora. Cora something or the other, I think is her name. Can't remember. She's local, but she's good. Paintings like that would look good at your hospital. Show everyone that you're an up and coming surgeon with an eye for the fine arts. Might improve business," he teased.

"Thank you, Mason, but I've done enough investing for one day," Horace answered, realizing that his wallet was considerably lighter than it had been a few minutes earlier. He quickly changed the subject. "Say, tell me about those fellows over there. I was watching them earlier and can't figure them out. They're doing something, but it doesn't look like they're sketching or painting. Looks like they're engraving something."

As they watched the young men they suddenly quit working, packed up their equipment, and wrapped up their project in paper. They hurried away, walking quickly toward one of the out buildings away from the lagoon. It seemed rather strange, but then Horace was still finding almost everything about Ox-Bow as rather strange. Too random, too lacking in organization.

"Could be. There's a small press down in the basement for print work. Maybe that's what they're doing. That interest you? Some nice etchings for the offices? They might be in the mood to sell some to you." Doctor Mason teased. Horace said nothing. They waited on the porch while Clarice helped Harriet wrap the paintings in butcher's paper to be carried home.

"I don't think so," Horace said flatly when he finally answered. "Just curious. Maybe it's time we think about heading back."

When the two women rejoined them, Horace said, "Now, Mrs. Walters, we left your Phoebe with Mrs. Garwood on the boat, so there is no telling what they're getting up to. My guess is that with Theo and Clarice here, and Doctor Mason, they're going to announce that we're all having dinner together. I'm sure they are counting on you joining us."

"We'll see," she answered, leading them back to Doctor Mason's car. "Tomorrow's the last day of class, so I've got to get some work done and cleaned up."

"You could help me pick a place in the library for these paintings," Horace replied gently. He hoped his offer would make amends. "And, I do hope you'll sign them before you pack up your brushes. I think you owe me that, don't you?"

A young woman rode up on a bicycle, panting, and her hair plastered against her face from perspiration. "Doctor Mason, I'm glad I caught you! Don't forget you're supposed to do the physicals at the Presbyterian camp tomorrow morning. Remember?"

"Good thing you caught me, Mae. Yeah, sure, we'll be there. Count on it. About nine or so. Usual time, right? " He answered. She jumped back on her bicycle and hurried back to the camp next door.

"You said, 'we'," Horace said bleakly.

"Of course! You two can come and join me. From what you said about that water pump, you're not going anywhere tomorrow. Besides, you'd miss all the fun of Venetian Night if you left early. You two can give me a hand, if you don't mind."

Before Horace could respond, Theo piped up, "Better in the exam room than the waiting room, right?"

"Just what am I getting talked into?" Horace asked.

"It's the camp next door. It's been owned by the Presbyterians out of Chicago for years, and they bring up youngsters from the tenements for a week of fresh air. Good food, exercise, fresh air, a little religion. All that fresh air and exercise in the wilderness stuff that Roosevelt was always talking about. Good stuff for a bunch of urchins from the tenements. Last day before they go back, they all get a physical. Just the basics. It isn't much, but it's more than their parents can afford back home. Sometimes a few of them come over here to see what it takes to be an artist. Probably it's the only chance they've ever had," Doctor Mason said.

"Well, those three fellows that were working over by that tree are from the camp next door. I understand they're Polish refugees," Mrs. Walters said quietly. "It can't be easy for them. I don't think they even speak English, and just keep to themselves. Maybe something good will come out of it."

"Speaking of people out here, Phoebe introduced me to the Episcopal vicar, and he said his wife was out here...." Horace began.

"Oh, her? Well, she is. It's a waste of her time and money, to say nothing of my time and effort. She hasn't any ability, no technique, no focus. Professionally speaking, not even good enough to be a Sunday afternoon painter. I think she just came out for a good time." Harriet said icily. "That's her coming out of the studio now. Looks like she's giving up early. I'm not surprised. She hasn't applied herself all week. She's the worst student I've ever had."

The woman walked quickly toward the car park to the side of the Old Inn and handed a package off to someone. Horace recognized the driver. It was the vicar. He put the car in gear and drove off.

"Strange couple," he thought. "Both of them. Good thing they're married to each other; it only spoils one marriage that way." He watched as the vicar drove back toward town while his wife walked up the trail that would eventually lead to the Crow's Nest. Doctor Horace was surprised, she was carrying another wrapped painting with her. He shook his head. Doctor Horace would never be able to understand artists.

CHAPTER THREE

On the whole, Saturday went quite well, with the exception of two brief but intense storms that swept over them at dinner and then much later. Until the evening, it was clear skies and good sailing. Even that bit of turbulence passed quickly.

A little before nine o'clock, Doctor Mason drove up in his Dodge touring car, and tapped the horn a couple of times to summon Horace and Theo. As soon as they were seated, Horace in the front, his brother in the back, Theo said, "You know, Mason, we came up here planning to take you up on your offer to spend the night at your cabin. But I got to tell you, Clarice and I are mighty glad to have slept on Horace's old scow. Did it ever occur to you that you have one bed in that glorified shack, and not enough room to sleep on the floor?"

Doctor Mason laughed, "Say, you know, I didn't even think of that." He continued to chuckle from time to time as they drove along Park Street to the corner where they turned to drive up to the Presbyterian Camp. "Now, if we were to go a bit farther, we'd be at the Oval Beach. Show it to you later, but right now, we've got our work to do." He parked the car near the dining hall and the three of them, medical bags in hand, got out. The director was waiting for them.

"Medical corps all present and accounted for, Sir!" Doctor Mason announced, saluting a thin young man by the name of Reverend Paths. His greeting startled and confused the youthful minister. "I'd like to introduce my two colleagues, Doctors Horace and Theodore

Balfour." The minister shook hands with all three, and then led them to the door of the main building.

He paused and turned around with a quizzical look on his face. "THE Doctors Balfour? Did I hear Doctor Mason correctly? THE Doctors Balfour? At my camp? Doing routine physicals?"

"That's us," Theo said. "Don't worry, we're a bit long in the tooth, but I think we remember the difference between a tongue depressor and a stethoscope." Horace grimaced at his brother's flippant comment, but added under his breath, "And a rubber mallet for reflexes, too."

"All right fellows. Here's the drill," Doctor Mason said as they set out their black leather bags on a table in the dining hall. "It's just like physicals back in our army days. The boys will line up. Each of them has a card with his name, age, height, and weight. Don't worry about names. I can't pronounce half the names of these Polish fellows. Some of them have more consonants than an eye chart. Height won't change, and if we're lucky they'll have put on a couple of pounds after a week here. We check eyes, ears, throat, and nose, and see if they have a heart beat and their breathing. A tap or two on each knee to check reflexes. And say, some of them think it's a real lark to try not to have a reflex and then kick out hard the last time. Watch out for them. Sing out the results to your assistant, and move on to the next boy."

"How many are we doing?" Theo asked.

"About three hundred this week. Crowded camp."

Theo let out a low whistle. "Hundred each. That'll keep us busy." He looked at the first boys coming through the door and thought, 'At least these boys aren't cannon fodder for the trenches. For which we can truly be thankful.' Then he repeated it out loud.

"Save the pulpit pounding for the reverend. Let's get to work," Horace growled. He knew his brother was right. He just didn't need to be reminded of the army camps of a decade ago. The thought of all those boys made him shudder.

"Better in the examining room than the waiting room, huh, Horace?" his brother asked. He was right about that, of course. A little work, something useful to do, was an improvement over sitting on his boat or wandering aimlessly through town. It even brought out a wintery smile in his older sibling.

Reverend Paths blew on his whistle to quiet the boys down. "All right, for those of you who have been here before, you know how this works. For you first-timers, shirts off. Move into three lines, and when it is your turn step up to one of the doctors. And knock off the horse place, would you please?" He waited until his young charges lined up, then blew his whistle again.

"Now, listen up. All of you. This is important. This is the last day of camp, and tomorrow you'll be going back home. But there's a special treat for you this evening. Saugatuck has a celebration they call Venetian Night. Tonight, at nine-thirty on the dot, everyone is to be in this building. Nine-thirty, and not a minute later. We're going to hike down to the river and watch the fireworks show. And then it's back here and straight to your bunks. Is that clear? What time?"

Several hundred young voices echoed off the room, "Nine-thirty!"

"Good. We'll ring the bell at eight to remind you. Now, physicals! You got lined up, so keep in your line, and keep the noise down." Reverend Paths nodded to the doctors that they could begin, and motioned the first three boys to move forward.

Theo was right. It was very much like the basic training camps back in 1917 and 1918. One boy after another stepped forward. A quick look in both ears, a quick check of the eyes, "Say, 'ah'" and the tongue depressor routine – left cheek, right cheek, under the tongue, then a quick check of heart and lungs with a stethoscope. "Good!" The boy put his card on the table to be marked by one of the camp employees, and was sent on his way. It was cursory, at best, but it was better than nothing.

They worked non-stop for close to two hours before the last camper was checked out. "We made fast work of it. I'd have been here all day if I'd done it on my own," Doctor Mason said. "You have no idea how grateful I am. Say, why don't I show you around the camp before I drive you back into town?"

Doctor Horace looked out the window and decided there wasn't all that much to see. Cabins, beach, water, and some three hundred noisy boys running around. "Perhaps another time, Mason," he said. "This old boy is ready for his nap."

"Hate to say it, but I agree with my brother. If it's all the same, I'm ready to go back, too," Theo yawned. "If you've seen one beach you've probably seen them all." He yawned again.

"All right, fellows. Have it your way, but you don't know what you're missing," Doctor Mason said. Horace didn't respond, but he was thinking that he wouldn't miss all that much.

On the drive back Doctor Mason said, "Well, I'll drop you fellows off at the boat, and then I'm going back up to my cabin for a while. Couple of things I want to do, and then I'll go back to Chicago later this afternoon or evening. I'm sure we'll cross paths at the College of Surgeons meeting in Philly this fall. Or, you get down to Chicago, let me know. We get visiting firemen all the time, and can show you a swell time. Chicago can be a real corker after dark, providing you know where to go, and trust me, I do."

"It's a little dangerous driving these roads after dark, isn't it?" Horace asked. Doctor Mason disagreed, telling them that about half the distance was paved, and besides that, he'd done it so often he could drive with his eyes closed.

"You'll miss the fireworks and Venetian Night," Theo added. Doctor Mason just shrugged. Compared to the Fourth of July in Chicago, these were fairly pathetic. "Take care, fellows. Safe travels back home in that old scow!" He waved and gunned the engine to cover up anything Horace might have said.

The brothers were just coming up the gangplank when Phoebe dashed out on deck and leaned over the rail to call to them. "Hurry up! Lunch is ready! Come and get it. Get washed up! Lunch is ready!"

"Hope the rest of the town doesn't think that's a general invitation," Theo laughed under his breath. "Wonder what Mr.s Garwood created this time?"

If Horace had hoped for fish, he was disappointed. Again. It was a cold buffet lunch – beef, vegetables, and worst of all, salad. He looked at it in disdain. "You know what the British call salad? Weeds. Weeds! They had the good sense not to eat the stuff until the war and food rationing. Then they had to eat weeds before a meal to fill them up. The French are worse. They think it's dessert!" He took his place at the table and glowered at the salad bowl.

"And we have dessert, too!" Phoebe sang out.

"Dessert at lunch? That's highly irregular," Horace said flatly.

"Yes!" the girl said. "Mrs Garwood said that you loooooove watermelon, so I asked Fred if he would drive me out to a farm just south of here where they raise melons, and I bought us one! Well, you bought us one, really. I think you owe Fred a dollar and seven cents for it."

"I see," Horace said solemnly. "If I am correct, you asked my driver to take you in my car down to a farm to buy a watermelon for my lunch that I am supposed to pay for?"

"That's right!" she said brightly.

Horace burst into laughter. "And I am sure that Mrs. Garwood told you that I am the best watermelon seed spitter in the entire country, and you want to have a contest. Am I right?"

"Right again, only I bet that I can beat you!"

"Slow down, young lady. I want to be sure I got this correct. Now, you say you asked my driver to take you in my car down to a farm?"

"Yes," she said.

"And was he a good driver?

"Oh yes! He's wonderful. He drove slowly through town so I could wave at everyone from the back seat."

"I see. And my car was comfortable enough for you, I hope."

"Oh yes, it's a wonderful car," she said.

Doctor Horace smiled and shook his head in approval. "Just checking to be sure it was up to your ladyship's standards."

Lunch on the deck was nearly over when Doctor Horace's attention was diverted as he watched a young delivery boy, probably from a ma and pa grocery store, stop at the gangplank of the boat directly behind the *Aurora*. He looked around warily to check the streets, lifted the bag out of the basket, and quickly closed the lid. He wasn't quite fast enough for Horace to miss it. At the bottom of the basket were two carefully wrapped bottles in brown paper. The boy cleverly hid them under the larger parcel. 'So, Frank Nitti wasn't just in Saugatuck on vacation. He had a nice little business going, complete with delivery service,' he thought to himself. 'No wonder that gangster was in town.'

He finished his lunch first and carried his plate into the galley. "And how was it, Doctor Horace?"

"Mrs. Garwood, as always the food was delicious. But why in the name of Hippocrates, Pasteur, and Rutherford B. Hayes do you serve beef at every single meal? My brother and I grew up on a farm and we ate beef. We ate bully and tinned beef chasing the Kaiser halfway across Europe. And here we are, in a state known around the world for their fish, their whitefish, Mrs. Garwood, and I haven't tasted it once since we got here! There must be a good explanation, but for the life of me I can't figure out why we don't have fish at least once! Would you explain this mystery to me, Mrs Garwood?"

The long-suffering woman went to the ice box and opened it, pointing at a shelf. "We're having fish tonight. We had the last of the beef today. Waste not want not was probably something you heard your mother say a thousand times. So did mine. Waste not want not. We finished the beef. You'll have your fish tonight! Now are you happy?"

"Thank you for clearing this up, Mrs. Garwood. Trust me, I am looking forward to something other than beef."

When he turned to leave the galley, she picked up a frying pan as if she was going to deck him with it, then burst out laughing. It wasn't often she could get the upper hand to put him in his place.

After the watermelon seed spitting contest which, to everyone's surprise, Clarice handily won, Horace announced he was going to take a long-awaited nap. The work done in the galley, and with nothing else to do, the Garwoods and Fred wandered into town, taking Phoebe along with them.

Horace went down to his cabin, closed and locked the door, and pulled the photograph of his wife out of the drawer and set it on the table next to his bed. He turned on his side to face it, and after a few minutes was fast asleep.

Truth be told, Horace was rarely in a sweet disposition when he wakened from an afternoon nap. Too many dreams from the past – the ghosts, as he called them, raced through his mind. The death of his wife, the war and all the young men who came through the field hospital, patients who had survived surgery and died or patients who died on the operating table. They haunted him, and waking up and reorganizing his thoughts came as a relief.

A while later that afternoon, the sight of his brother and Clarice, along with Phoebe, caught his attention. All three of them were coming up the sidewalk carrying sticks and long tubes over their shoulders. Doctor Horace put on his glasses to have a better look. He growled under his breath. "What in thunderation are you carrying?" he demanded as they arrived at the gangplank.

"Congreve rockets!" Theo said. "Sky rockets, they call them now. Same difference, really. I thought we might have our own show." He was smiling broadly.

"Won't that be fun!" Phoebe added.

"Young lady, your mother is not going to approve!" he said firmly at her.

"I know," she laughed.

"Theo, just whose idea was this?" his brother asked.

"Oh, all mine!" he said.

"Of course. I'm sure it was. It wouldn't surprise me if you were talked into it by a certain precocious young lady. And it looks like you got a bag of lady-fingers in your pocket, too. All right, take them down and put them in the store room as far away from the engine room as possible. And then lock the door. Between a bad boiler and fireworks the *Aurora* is turning into a death trap!" Horace was still irritable, and his mood was not improving.

"And, I see I have some visitors," he added, looking past his brother at the two men who had come along with them.

"Say, that's right. I almost forgot. I'd like you to meet a couple of friends of mine. This is a long time friend, Trix. Well, TM, as he's properly called. TM Justus. We met in Paris right after the war. Trix was a corporal in one of the bands, and after he got out, well, he stayed on for a while..."

"A bit like you, Theo," Horace reminded him.

"Yeah, a bit like me. And F. Scott Fitzgerald and some short story writer named Hemingway. Whole bunch of us staying on to see what we were fighting for. Now Trix here organized a band of his own. He put together a jazz band to introduce American music to the Frenchies at this watering hole owned by a fellow named Harry. That's where we met up with Gerald and Sarah Murphy, and they took Trix down to the Riviera to play that winter in the hotels.

"Before you say anything to insult him, he's also the French horn player for the NBC Orchestra out of Chicago. Radio, just in case you're falling behind here. Classical musician.

"And with him, let me introduce you to Ollie Anderson. He's got the Blackhawk Orchestra that's playing at the Big Pavilion this week."

Trix interrupted, "We're old friends, and I'm sitting in, playing brass while their regular horn player is off getting married."

"Theo, is this going anywhere, or am I being invited to some sort of ad hoc army reunion?" Horace asked irritably.

"I'm getting to that. You know how I've always thought we should have a town band to play down in Eccles Park? A park band. Well, I think Trix is our man. He has the summer off from the radio, and he could come up and be the director. Next year. It's too late this year. What do you think?"

"On the whole, I'd say that music is a distraction from work. I don't mind some good American marches – Sousa, Fillmore, and that type. But I don't see any point in having that wild jazz foisted on people anymore than it already is. Besides, they've got that at the Armoury."

"If I can say something," Trix interrupted. "I'll be square with you. I like jazz, but if I'm being hired to lead a park band and you want more traditional pieces, then we'll be playing traditional pieces.

Horace nodded in approval. "Look, I don't want to be rough on you about this. But Eccles is a clean town. A clean, church going, hard working, honest, Republican-voting town. I want to see it stay that way. It's good for our hospital, and what's good for our hospital is good for Eccles. Simple as that. If, and I'm saying more than if, you come up to direct a summer park band, that's the way it's going to be. Otherwise, you'll be on the first train back to Chicago. You might want to think about it for a while, and we'll talk later."

"That's good to know. You see, what I have in mind is a town band. A band made up of your own men and women, maybe some of your own employees. Now, you agree, don't you, that if a fellow is blowing on a horn they can't be blowing their money down at some speakeasy. And if they're practicing with a band, they'll come to work with a clear head," Trix countered.

"You can count on Trix," Ollie said. "If he gives you his word, he'll keep his word. But I'll tell you what. Why don't you at least give us a chance. Come on over to the pavilion tonight and tell the girl at the ticket desk I invited you. I'll speak to her when we get back. Come over and listen, just for a while, and see what you think. There's a chance you might change your mind."

"We'll see," Horace said. He shook hands with the two musicians then exiled himself in his library. His afternoon was not going well. "Sky rockets and jazz musicians, what's next?" he muttered as he sat down and picked up a Sherlock Holmes mystery. He stayed there, reading, for the next hour, losing himself on the Dartmouth Moors and a ferocious hound.

He would have finished the book if Fred hadn't knocked on the door. "You got a minute, Doc?" he asked. Horace motioned him to come in.

Fred got straight to the point. "I went off on my own for a while after Doctor Theo ran into some friends. Just a little scouting around. Anyway, north of town there's some vacant land and I saw four big trucks parked there. I was sort of curious and crept in close-like. Thought you'd want to know that Nitti and some of his mates were there, unloading the trucks into a couple of shacks."

"Bootlegging?" Doctor Horace asked.

"Bootlegging," Fred answered firmly. "That's what I figured so I just stayed out of sight and watched for a while. Before long, a couple of fellows came up with a truck and loaded them into their truck and drove off back towards town. About twenty minutes or so, and they're back for another load. I took off while they were loading up again and walked back.

"Sure enough, they're behind me, so I stuck out my thumb for a lift and they gave me a ride. Asked if I'd like to make a buck helping them unload some stuff: ' garden fresh produce' they called it, into the South America. And another buck to keep quiet about it."

"Is this story going anywhere?" Doctor Horace asked irritably.

"Nothing more than I thought you'd be wanting to know how Nitti gets his booze into Chicago. Canada to Detroit, Detroit over to here, and then down to Chicago on the cruise ships. Nice little racket they got going on around here. Sort of surprising for a little place like Saugatuck," Fred said.

"I don't see how this has much to do with us, Fred," Doctor Horace said.

"Me, neither. Except I was thinking, if that's what he's doing here, maybe he's got a little something going on back to home we don't know about. I just figured you'd want to be one up on Nitti." Fred was barely whispering.

"Point well made. Good to know. We'll keep it in mind and keep our eyes and ears open." Doctor Horace nodded, and Fred took it to mean that it was time for him to leave.

Mrs. Walters' afternoon had taken more effort and energy than she expected, and it left her tired. It was the last day of art classes, and most of the students would be leaving, only to be replaced by a new class. She would be quite happy to see the end of that lazy and inattentive Mrs. Smith. Those who were staying on for a second week or the rest of the summer, couldn't focus much better. They were supposed to do their critiques, but were more interested in Venetian Night, the fireworks, and the dance at the Big Pavilion. It had left her exhausted, trying to do her work while her students were less than interested and completely distracted. Worse than getting Phoebe to memorize her times table or spelling words for class. 'Thank goodness for Sylvia,' she thought, then remembered that she was one of the older students. Sylvia seemed to be committed to being a successful artist.

She finished at Ox-Bow, rode her bike down to the chain ferry, and then home to freshen up. She splashed some cold water on her face to revive. At least she remembered to bring along a tube of black paint and a fine brush. She still had the paintings to sign. One last look in the mirror. Acceptable. Presentable. Blue mid-length dress, black shoes. No hat. A good example to her daughter, or so she tried to convince herself. She didn't want to admit that she wanted to make a good impression on Doctor Theo. More importantly, a good impression on Clarice. She turned around and dabbed on a drop of scent behind each ear, and another drop on her left wrist, then rubbed it against her right.

"Permission to come aboard?" she asked from the foot of the gangplank when she spotted Gar. He waved her up.

"Doc's in his library. I'd knock first. He's sort of testy. Least wise, he was. He'll be glad to see you, you know," the captain said. Gar was right. Horace was happy to see here.

"Mrs. Garwood, that is not fish!" Horace said firmly. "I distinctly remember seeing some fresh white fish in the ice box, and clearly remember you saying that we were having fish for dinner this evening." He sat at the table on the deck looking at serving dishes laden with frankfurters and buns, baked beans, and sweet corn on the cob. The others were already at their places when he and Mrs Walters came on deck and he stared down at the table.

"Yes, you did see fish, Doctor Horace, and you'll be having fish tomorrow night," Mrs. Garwood said with equal firmness. "Phoebe thought it would be more fun to have a picnic on a boat. She's never had a picnic on a boat before, you know. Now, surely you wouldn't begrudge a nice young girl a new experience, would you?"

"No. No, of course not," he answered, his lips firmly set.

"And, we're having watermelon ala mode!" Phoebe added.

"Ice crème and watermelon together?" her mother asked. "That's rather strange, dear."

"Oh, it was a brand new recipe I thought up all on my own. Doctor Horace likes ice crème and watermelon, so I thought we could have them together!"

"Well, two new first time experiences at one meal," Horace said grimly. "Tuck in before the beans get cold and the ice crème melts." He felt Clarice kick him under the table, reminding him to behave like an adult and not a spoiled child.

Dinner started off a bit rough, moved into smooth sailing through the main course, and then sailed straight into a heavy squall near the end. This time, neither Doctor Horace nor Mrs. Walters had anything to do with it.

"Ahoy, the boat!" a voice shouted from the sidewalk below. "Hiya, Teddy and Horace old boy! It's me, your ol' pal Frank! Gotta little somethin' for youse two!"

Theo and Horace looked at each other, and in unison whispered, "Nitti." Horace pushed back his chair and threw down his napkin on the seat in disgust to go to the rail to speak to him. Capone's enforcer and a couple of grinning young gangsters, all of them looking the worse for drink, were waiting for them.

"Hiya, Horace, ol' pal. Say, I got a flask here. A little pick you up. Wan' some? Say, I got another one in this pocket, and there's plenty more where this comes from!" He started to make his way, very unsteadily, up the gangplank. "Enough for all of youse."

"Get off and go away, Frank. You're not wanted here!" Horace shouted down at him. "It's a private party."

"But Horace, Teddy, I'm your ol' pal Frank. Frank, the life of the party!"

"It's a private party, and you're not invited. Now, stay off my boat and just get on down the street."

"Ah, have it your way, then. But youse don' know whatcher missin'," he said, swaying unsteadily on the sidewalk.

"On your way, Nitti," Doctor Horace repeated, pointing down the sidewalk.

"All right, all right, Doc. Frank Nitti knows when he's not wanted!" He put the hip flask back in his jacket and started unevenly down the street.

In less than two minutes of Frank Nitti, the black storm clouds of anger and fury settled over the dinner party. "I'm surprised by the friends you keep, Doctor Balfour," Mrs. Walters said quietly, angrily. "A good friend, a VERY good friend, from the way he was speaking to you. I'm surprised and disgusted!" She threw down her fork in anger, bouncing it off the table. "And all the more since I entrusted Phoebe to your care. And now I find out you're friends, consorting openly with that, that, that, murdering gangster!"

Doctor Horace remained calm. His voice was pure ice. "He is certainly no friend of mine, nor my brother, nor our families. In our profession we meet all sorts of people. As physicians we treat all people without regard to any circumstances."

"I see. Well, I have no hesitation choosing my friends wisely, and especially around Phoebe. We're leaving. Now!" She wiped a drop of spit from her lip.

She had gone too far. "Sit down, please, Mrs. Walters, before you make a spectacle of yourself," Doctor Horace said. She didn't move. He repeated, "Sit down!"

She stared in fury at him, but took her seat.

"Yes, I know Frank Nitti, and I know what sort of man he is. So does my brother and Mrs. Balfour. We all know. The whole nation knows what he and his gang are like. He has been a patient for the past few years. I've doctored other criminals just like him and maybe worse. And during the war I doctored Germans who a few hours earlier had probably killed some of our Doughboys. I don't like treating criminals like Nitti, anymore than I liked treating the Hun, but I took an oath.

"But Nitti isn't the worst of them. You know who's worse? Bankers. Eastern bankers and railroad owners, and the men who control the stockyards in Chicago. Oh, they wear a better cut of suit and drink a more expensive bottle of whiskey, and they know how to deport themselves, at least in public. They know a bread knife from a steak knife, and they'll turn right around and put either of them into the back of every small town merchant, farmer, and rancher. They get away with it, too. You know how? They don't use a gun. They charge interest, sometimes as high as twenty-two percent. Now, there's a criminal for you.

"You might want to take a look around this town, too. This afternoon I watched a delivery boy from the local store. You know what he had in his bicycle basket? Bootleg booze that's being sold under the counter or out of the pantry right here in Saugatuck.

"And another thing, someone around here has got a real nice sweetheart deal at the colliery down the river a bit. Every commercial steamer that comes and goes has to fill up with coal before they leave. You know why? They make the steamers take on coal whether they need it or not so that they can buy it in large quantities. And then they can sell it to you and everyone else cheaper that way. So the next time you light your cook stove or fill the stoker down in the basement, it seems to me that you're in on it too.

"Mrs. Walters, the world isn't all nicey-nicey and pretty little paintings! You can put that in your pipe and smoke it." Doctor Balfour stood up and threw his linen napkin on his chair. "I don't know about the rest of you, but I'm going for a walk, preferably alone!"

He stalked down the length of the deck to go down the gangplank, and turned the opposite direction from Nitti.

Phoebe was stunned. Her lip began to tremble, and she got up from the table to stand at the rail and watch her friend as he went down the street. 'Oh, that's not good,' she thought. "His boater is on straight.'

The girl wasn't the only one shocked by Doctor Horace's outburst. The unflappable Clarice collected herself and took charge as she often did when her brother-in-law had gone too far. "Well, the normal thing to do is have fireworks after dark. It looks like we have an early start. What a surprise. Phoebe, be a dear and go have a walk with Horace. He'd welcome that very, very much. You're the one person he will welcome. Go! And Theo, be a dear and go find something to do somewhere else. Harriet and I are going to sit here for a few minutes and have a quiet word."

The two women sat in silence, and then Clarice reached over to take Harriet's hands. "I think I told you yesterday, sometimes it seems like half my life is spent smoothing over feathers Horace ruffles. Sometimes he does it to Theo. Sometimes another doctor, or almost anyone. But there are many things you don't know about him. Maybe he doesn't know them himself. More likely, he knows his faults all too well, but he keeps everything bottled up, and with a tight cork on it. Horace wasn't always like that, but he's been hurt too many times. The war changes men. It did for my Theo and it did for Horace, just in different ways. And then his wife died, his daughter married and moved away to follow her husband, and there was more than we don't..... Well, a son who died. And now he's getting old and feeling shoved aside. Theo's the same, but at least he's got ...."

"You?" Harriet asked quietly.

"Yes. Yes, that. I know I'm good for him. And he's got things that interest him. Horace was different from the beginning. Driven, hard working. Building up his medical practice, and his family. Always the leader. That didn't change after the war. But now that his family is pretty much gone, and he's winding down medicine. It's hard on him. He bottles it up more and more, and won't let anyone get close to him. All he ever wanted was to be a small town doctor, but things didn't turn out that way."

"But your Theo is so different?" Harriet asked.

"He's wounded in his own way. He just bandages himself differently. It was the war. They were both surgeons just behind the front. So many boys shredded by bullets and shells, or their lungs burned out by gas. They couldn't save them all, and they felt bad for some who pulled through.

"Theo and Horace got discharged the same day. Horace got on the first boat he could find out of France, and so he never got the telegram that his wife had died of the flu. Not until he got home, and by then she was already buried. Between that and the war...."

"And your Theo?"

"Theo wrote that he needed to stay on. He wanted to do what he could to help out. Of course, when he found out about Horace's wife, it was too late to be with his brother. That was rough on him because they've always been close. Oh, they scrap like any two brothers, but never try to wedge in between them. Theo took it hard that he'd let Horace down. Between what he saw in the war and then Horace's wife's death, well, let's just say, he got a little lost. After all that he wanted to feel alive again. That's why he didn't come home right away. I can't blame him. He needed it. And thank goodness he got it out of his system before he did come home. Before he did get back to the States, back when he was in France, when he wasn't volunteering at a hospital, he was hanging around with musicians and writers. All of the Doughboys who'd been to hell and back. A couple of his old army mates were here this afternoon, in fact. They spent their time drinking champagne and coffee until they burned the war out of them. And then he came home.

"Horace hated that in Theo. Theo decided to live, while Horace retreated from life. I sometimes think he tried to work himself to death. I really do. But he couldn't bring himself to go the distance. Sometimes the only time he becomes human again is when he is on this old boat.

"And there is one more thing I want you to hear. I've never seen him warm up to another person like he has to your Phoebe. When she is around, he's his old self again, like he was before the war. And for what your daughter has given him, Harriet, I am truly, truly grateful."

Clarice let go of Harriet's hand to find a handkerchief. Both women were crying.

Mrs. Walters didn't say anything. She got up and slowly walked the length of the boat pacing it twice, thinking over everything Clarice had told her. For a while she rested one hand on the rail, staring down at the gangplank. and then followed her daughter on the sidewalk. Tears came again when she saw Phoebe and Doctor Balfour walking slowly hand in hand back to the *Aurora*. She picked up her pace to meet up to them.

"I am sorry. I am so, so sorry. I was rude. I was wrong. I don't care if you won't forgive me, but just know I am so, so very, very sorry. Please. Just know I am so very sorry." Harriet was standing in front of Horace, tears still flowing down her cheeks as she looked at him.

"And I was rude and mean, too. I didn't mean to blow up at you, Mrs.... Harriet," he said quietly. It surprised him when he reached out to take both her hands. He knew he was doing it awkwardly, but he knew words were not enough.

"We've both been hurt. Hurting each other doesn't make it any better," she said, trying to smile as she looked up at him.

He nodded silently in agreement. She scared him, the way she could break through his defences.

Phoebe took it all in, watching them look at each other so long she wondered when they would get all mushy and hug.

"Start over?" Horace offered.

"Start over," she nodded.

Phoebe let out a long, loud sigh. "Come on! We still have more watermelon ala mode!" She said brightly.

Clarice cried again as she saw the three of them returning to the ship. Phoebe and Horace were walking hand in hand. Harriet was resting her hand on his arm. She looked up to the sky. "Thank you! Thank you!"

Doctor Horace shocked everyone when he announced they were all going to the Big Pavilion to hear the Blackhawk Orchestra. It was the only thing he could do to make amends.

"All of us?" Theo asked.

"All of us. You and Clarice. The Garwoods, Fred, Harriet and Phoebe, and me."

"You, too?" Theo asked a second time.

"Yes. And don't sound so surprised."

They walked down to the dance hall. "Wonder what's come over my brother? Theo asked his wife.

"I'd say Horace met his Waterloo," Clarice whispered back.

"Brains and beauty. I don't know what to say."

"Then I'd keep quiet if I were you and don't spoil anything. Just let it be."

"From what Trixie and Ollie told you about their music, I never thought you'd darken the door," Theo practically shouted to Horace over the noise of the crowd. "Not your sort of music."

"No! Certainly isn't. Not at all. Do they have to play that loudly?"

"It's all the fashion today. Welcome to 1928!" He was going to keep Horace company, but Clarice had other ideas. She pulled him toward the dance floor, leaving Horace with Harriet and Phoebe. Moments later Phoebe went over to where the Gardwoods were standing, and led the captain out to the dance floor. Seeing her standing alone, Horace was about to step towards Mrs. Garwood when Royce the stoker led her into the crowds. He felt stranded with Harriet. They watched as the music changed from the Charleston to the Black Bottom, and back to the Charleston again. And then Ollie Anderson shouted into the microphone that they were going to do a new song by Irving Berlin called "Monkey Doodle Do." The crowd applauded. The music started again.

"A bit scandalous, don't you think?" Harriet shouted at him.

"Definitely. But then, back in my day, we scandalized our parents when we did the Hesitation Waltz." He was smiling as he remembered the way his mother and father fussed and complained about what they thought was immoral and wicked music, and couples dancing face to face instead of a stately promenade.

"You? You danced? Seriously?"

"Not seriously. Badly. Very badly!"

"Well, come on then!" Harriet tugged him by the hand out to the floor.

"Twenty-three skidoo!" Phoebe cheered. "Twenty-three skidoo!"

Harriet understood what he meant when he said he danced badly. Twice she winced when he stepped on her toes. It didn't stop her.

It had been years since she had danced, and never since Phoebe had been born. She wasn't giving up over a squished toe. Not that she was much better. Twice she stepped on his toes by accident.

"Cutting in, Big Brother," Theo said, tapping Horace on the shoulder. "I'm saving her from needing major surgery on some broken foot bones."

Horace turned toward his sister-in-law, but she shook her head. "No, Horace. My feet are just fine and I'd like them to stay that way."

Horace was relieved he was sitting out Berlin's tune, "Always." Too slow and the dancers crushed themselves against their partners.

A little after ten, Ollie Anderson brought the music to a stop. He shouted in his megaphone, "We're going to take a little break so all you folks can go out and see the fireworks. And then we'll be right back up here on the stage for the second half!"

"I think that's our cue to go back to the boat and watch the fireworks," he told Phoebe and Harriet.

"What about the others? Shouldn't we wait for them?" Phoebe asked.

"They're big enough to find their own way home. Come on, let's get the best spot to watch the show!"

The crowd poured out of the Big Pavilion and onto the streets. "Oh look!" Phoebe said. "Some of the boats are decorated with Japanese lanterns! Isn't it beautiful?" She was about to add that it was too bad the *Aurora* wasn't festooned, but she thought better of it.

From the west side of the river a solitary rocket whistled through the air, leaving behind a trail of smoke and sparks, and then exploded and sent a blast reverberating through the valley. There was a long wait, and the show began in earnest. Phoebe jumped up and down in excitement, then plugged her ears just before the explosion. The three of them, along with the crowds along the waterway, oohhed and ahhed each time another shell burst over the water.

"What about ours?" Phoebe asked after the grand finale. "Aren't we going to light ours tonight, too?"

She was yawning, and was weepy-tired.

"I think we'll save ours until tomorrow night. How does that sound? Besides, it looks to me like the Sandman has already visited you, young lady."

"Tomorrow, for real? You promise?"

"I promise," Doctor Horace said. He spit in his right palm and slammed his left fist into it. "Deal!"

He glanced at Mrs. Walters, almost relishing the look of utter disdain and horror on her face.

"I taught Doctor Horace how to do it!" Phoebe said in triumph.

"I see," her mother replied, none too pleased. "All right, Phoebs, time to go home and get tucked into bed. Doctor Horace, thank you. For everything." She made a motion to reach for his hand to squeeze it, then thought better of it, and wrapped her arm around her daughter's shoulder to pull her closer to her.

"Tomorrow?" he asked.

"Tomorrow," Harriet told him.

He leaned over the railing to watch them walk back to their home. Far away, the Blackhawk Orchestra was playing the Charleston.

When mother and daughter were out of sight, he retreated to his library to continue reading the mystery he had started earlier. He finished the novel just as the Blackhawk Band played its final piece, "The End of a Perfect Day." It was an old piece, and even for a music non-lover, he knew the melody and words from his past. "Indeed it has been," he whispered to himself as he turned off the light over his chair.

CHAPTER FOUR

It was well after two the next morning when Gar, looking ridiculous in his yellow rain slicker pulled over his pyjamas, pounded on Doctor Horace's cabin door. "Doc, wake up! Wake up! There's some sort of emergency!" he shouted.

"What in thunderation? What sort of an emergency? Someone hurt? Who? Horace asked as he struggled to his feet and paused to straighten out his pyjamas before opening the door.

"Don't know. All I know is that the police chief said there's an emergency and for me to get you and Doctor Theo, and tell you to bring your bags along with you. Oh, and to make it snappy. That's what he said, 'snappy'. I got better manners than that."

"All right. Go wake Theo. I'll meet him up on deck."

"The chief, Callie, wants you right away!" a man shouted from the sidewalk. "Where's your brother? I'm supposed to bring him along, too!"

"He's coming," Doctor Horace answered. "What sort of an emergency is it?"

"Don't know for sure. Looks like something has happened to that Episcopal preacher man up to the All Saints Church. It's not for me to say. Chief Callie can tell you. All he's told me is to come down here and fetch you two saw-bones."

A few minutes later Horace and Theo squeezed into a small pickup truck with the driver. None of them talked on the short drive down Water Street and onto Butler. They pulled up in front of city hall. "Best go on inside. Callie's waiting," the driver said. "I gotta go up and stand guard. Leastwise, it's not raining."

"Yeah, that's something," Theo said. He wasn't fully awake yet. "I thought we were past night duty once we got past being interns," he added, looking in Horace's direction. His brother wasn't listening.

"Well, what we got here is him stone cold dead. Well, he aint exactly cold just yet, so it didn't happen too long ago." Callie said as the Balfour brothers looked at the body stretched out on a desk. "Found him dead-like, face down in front of his parsonage. I can't tell if it was an accident, natural causes, or foul play murder. Normally, I'd handle this sort of thing myself, but then I thought to myself, 'Callie, we got a couple of world-famous doctors in town; better let the experts handle it.' Besides, the mayor'ld be real sore if I didn't call you to lend a hand."

"All right. We need some room to work, and hold that desk lamp up so we can see what we're doing," Horace instructed the chief. "At least you've got electricity here."

The brothers stood on opposite sides of the desk, working their way down his body from the head, making a careful examination. All the while they talked quietly to each other. "No sign of a knife wound.... No bruises on the forehead.... He's not bleeding from the ears or nose.... Ribs haven't been damaged." They opened his shirt. They looked for a knife wound on his neck, but there wasn't one. No bruising on the chest. "Callie, you sure he was face down when you found him?" Theo asked.

"Yup, face down."

"That's interesting. Strange. No bleeding from the nose or ears," Horace observed. "No bleeding from the mouth or cut lips."

"What does that mean?" Callie asked. The brothers ignored his question. They continued to ignore him when he asked the question a second time.

The three men carefully rolled him over, Horace giving instructions the entire time, and then the Balfours began their exam again, this time starting at the feet. They slowly worked their way up to the deceased's head, finding nothing out of the ordinary.

"Wait a second. This might be interesting," Theo said, reaching into a pocket for a pen to push apart the man's hair. "Looks like a blow to the back of the head." Horace looked more closely, his nose inches from the hair Theo had moved to one side.

"Nice clean job of it. A blow to the cerebral cortex. Instantaneous death. That's why there was no bleeding," Horace said, standing up and stretching his back.

"That's what I saw, too," Theo added.

"Blow to the back of a head with a blunt instrument," Callie said, almost pleased that he had a murder case on his hands.

"Not quite," Doctor Horace answered. "Theo, take a look from over here. Move that light in closer, would you Callie?." Horace took the pen to hold the hair in place while his brother moved next to him, and examined the head more closely. "Singed!"

Theo got his medical bag and pulled out some small forceps and a magnifying glass. "What do you think, Horace?"

"Looks like old-fashioned wadding. That's strange."

"What do you mean 'wadding'?" Callie demanded.

"Wadding. Cotton or paper used in a black powder gun. Pour the powder in, put the ball or slug in some wadding to tighten the seal, and tamp it down. Wadding. It's wadding. No doubt in my mind. Little burnt shards of it. No mistake," Horace explained.

"But there's no bullet hole!" Callie complained.

"No. No there isn't. Whoever did this knew exactly what they were doing. It's not just murder. It's an execution. The concussion at close range would have been more than enough to kill him. Execution. Whoever did this has done this sort of work before," Horace said.

"Why a black powder gun and not a pistol?" Callie asked, sitting down hard on a chair.

"My guess is that this was done during the fireworks show. Rigor mortis hasn't set in, so that would fit in with the timing. They use black powder in their display. Plus, every boy in town was lighting off fire crackers of their own. The sound would have blended right in, and nobody would have noticed. It gave them more time to get away."

"I've never heard of such a thing," Callie objected. "Why not use a slug to be sure they got the job done? Doesn't make sense."

"Well, it's similar to what Capone and his men do when they want to be quiet about it. Only, they use a bar of soap in a sock, then slip up behind their victim, and whack! Instant death. All they have to do is toss the soap away one place and the sock somewhere else." Theo said. "That's where they get the term 'whacking someone'". Dr Horace stretched his back.

"My guess is that they were hoping you wouldn't notice it and just say he died of natural causes," Theo added.

"Say, one of Capone's boys, that Frank Nitti, he's in town! I'll bet he's got his hands into this!" Callie said with excitement.

"Chief, you know, I don't want to tell you how to run your department, but I'll bet you a bag of apples and another bag of donuts that he doesn't have anything to do with it. It's not his style. A pistol, lead pipe, baseball bat, maybe even a knife. But now an old fashioned black powder gun? Never. Not even in a small town like this." Horace told him.

"Just the same, I've got to do my duty. I want to see what he knows."

"You're wasting your time, Chief." He repeated.

He ignored the two doctors and went to the door to call one of his men. "Nitti's staying down to the Butler, top floor. Go down and roust him out and haul him in here on the double. And bring anyone else you see, too. I want to get his particulars about his whereabouts tonight and see what he has to say about this," he told one of his men.

"I tell you, you're off on a wild goose chase. And losing time catching the real killer," Horace said. His temper was rising.

The chief stared at them, silent for a few moments, before he began. "Seems to me you two are pretty quick to stand up for Nitti. For all I know, you two might have come up here pretending to be on a vacation jaunt just to have a little meeting with him or something like that. Yeah, now that I think of it, that's a real possibility. You two in cahoots with Nitti and Capone, thinking you could pull a fast one on a small town cop." Callie was flushed with anger or excitement. "I'm going to talk with Nitti and then mull that one over."

"You just do that, Chief. Meanwhile, my brother and I are going to get some sleep. You just have your little chit-chat with Frank Nitti, and mull that over. You might even come to your senses," Horace snapped at him.

"Yeah, I'll let you go back to your boat. But you're gonna have to be back here first thing in the morning. I'm gonna call the coroner over in Allegan first thing, and I want you fellows around when he gets here."

"Why don't you call him now?" Theo asked.

"Can't."

"Too busy chasing Nitti," Horace muttered.

"Bobbie shuts down the switchboard at ten, and I don't want to wake her up in the middle of the night, even if she could ring through to the coroner," Callie said.

"Your switchboard closes at ten?" Horace asked, his eyebrows arched in surprise.

"Yeah, lot of folks don't have a phone. Don't see much point in it. And around here, good decent folks go to bed early so it's just a waste of time having her sit there at the switchboard knitting or what not."

Horace shook his head in disgust.

The Balfours picked up their bags and walked back to the boat. For the first block they didn't say anything. Horace chortled. "You happen to notice that Callie had the body on the desk in the mayor's office? Hope he's not squeamish about having a body on his blotting paper."

Theo was the more serious one this time. "You know, this doesn't make much sense."

"Which part?"

"None of it makes much sense. Killing a minister, especially the way they did it...."

"No, it makes sense. At least it did to whoever killed him, at the time. Murder always makes sense. We're just not in on the secret. Anyway, it's not our problem. We pronounced him dead and gave the chief the cause of death. Up to Callie to take it from there. Think you can get back to sleep?" Horace asked.

"Don't know. You know we're going to be stuck here for a day or so. Maybe longer, especially if that Callie thinks we have something to do with it," Theo said.

"Ah, he's talking crazy talk, all excited, but you're right. I'm still sitting in the waiting room. Thunderation!"

"Pretty nice waiting room. Pretty nice people to wait with, too." He glanced at Horace to see if he understood the meaning. If his brother caught his meaning, he intentionally ignored it.

"Want something to help you nod off? Horace asked when they got to the *Aurora*.

"Prescription?"

"Yeah. Wrote the prescription myself. There's a bottle of single malt in the library, as prescribed by a certified medical doctor."

"You sly old dog, you! And here's me thinking you were law-abiding," he teased.

Horace poured them each a small glass and they settled into old leather club chairs. "That Callie is a piece of work, chasing after Nitti like that," he said flatly.

"Ah, the old fellow wants to play the big shot, that's all," Theo answered. "Probably the most exciting thing that's happened in his whole life."

"Yeah, and while he's off on that he's letting the real murderer get away. A real Ford Sterling and his Keystone Cops, if you ask me."

"You got a better idea?"

"Well, one. For one thing, did you notice who wasn't around? The wife. Mrs Smith."

Theo's face dropped in surprise. He hadn't thought of her, either. "You think she did it?" he finally sputtered.

"Don't know. But Callie didn't even notice or mention her. And, she wasn't there. I doubt she was there when someone found the body. If she'd been at the vicarage Callie would have said something or brought her in for questioning. Doesn't make a lick of sense. No, Callie didn't even think about her."

"You could have said something, you know," Theo answered.

"To that cloth-head? There wasn't much point in it. He wanted to get the bragging rights for arresting Frank Nitti."

"Callie wouldn't be the first on that account. You think we ought to go back and tell him?"

"Not much point in it. By now he's got Nitti down to City Hall and probably trying to figure out how to plug in the bright lights to give him the third degree. Rubber hoses, brass knuckles, the whole business." Horace finished his drink and put the glass on a book shelf. "Anyway, I don't know about you, but I'm going to bed. You ought to do the same, too. Don't forget, we have to report for duty in a couple of hours."

Theo got up, ready to go to his cabin, then turned around. "Horace, you think Callie even checked the house, took a look inside?"

Horace gave him a blank look. "Thunderation! I doubt he did look to see if she was dead or wounded inside. Or the church, for that matter. Thunderation! He stood up to open the secret compartment in the book case and pulled out a revolver. He checked the cylinder, then slipped it into his pocket. "Let's go. Bring your bag. If she is there and wounded...."

"You think we'll need that?" Theo asked, looking at his brother's pocket. Horace didn't respond.

There was a faint sliver of light in the east as they walked up the hill toward All Saints', and only the sound of a single robin. The brothers remained silent as they walked, both of them lost in their thoughts. "Church first?" Horace asked.

"Think it's unlocked?" Theo asked when they got to the front door.

"Phoebe said they never lock it. Just put your shoulder to it." Theo pushed it open, the hinges creaking, and the latch on the inner door rattled as they opened it. "Well, they'll know we're here," Horace said grimly.

"A little dark in here. Think they've got candles or something?" Theo asked.

"It's a church! Of course they've got candles!" Horace felt his way down the centre aisle to the altar, and removed two tall tapers. He handed them to his brother and found a box of matches.

"Think it's all right to use them? I mean, they're holy or something, aren't they?"

"Then don't tell anyone," Horace said.

The two men slowly walked up and down the side aisles, checking every pew, and under them, all the time with Horace holding on to the pistol still in his pocket, ready to produce it, should it come to that.

Nothing. They didn't know whether that was good or bad news. Good, if only that they didn't find a body or a sign of struggle. To be thorough, they changed sides and made a second inspection, then both of them worked their way down the centre aisle, looking from a different angle.

"Think we ought to check the house?" Theo asked after they blew out the flames and put the candles back in place. Horace nodded in agreement. They slipped out the church door and walked over to the vicarage.

"Thought I heard someone say Callie had posted a night watchmen on the place," Theo whispered. "Wonder where he is?"

"Probably down to the station working Nitti over. Anyway, no one's here."

The doors were locked tight.

There was nothing more they could do, and both of them knew there was nothing more they should do. It was a matter for Callie, no matter how incompetent he might be.

They walked back to the *Aurora* and finally got to bed.

"What was it?" Clarice yawned loudly as she asked her husband.

"Emergency. I'll tell you later," he yawned and closed his eyes. He was too tired to start a long conversation and two additional questions from her for every answer he gave. And she was too accustomed being married to a doctor who kept strange hours to pry.

They slept for a couple of hours before Callie was outside the boat, shouting for them. When they didn't come fast enough, he reached in through the truck window to blow on the horn.

"As soon as I'm shaved and dressed," Horace told him. He took his time, refusing to be rushed by the police chief.

"We'll drive down to the Maplewood. Bobbie should be there by now and she'll place the call. Then we'll go back to City Hall 'cause I got a lot a questions to ask you two," Callie said.

"I'm sure you do. And I've got a few for you, as well," Horace told him.

"Yeah, well, at least you two got a good night's sleep. I've been up all night with Nitti. He's a tough nut. Couldn't get him to confess to anything. Said he had an alibi on account of the fact that he was at the Big Pavilion all night until they closed. We checked, and the janitor said he was. Course, Nitti could have bribed him. And here's the kicker: You know who he said he was with? You know who? Your driver, that's who! I'll want a word with him, too."

Bobbie put the call through, emphasizing to the operator on the other end that it was "LONG DISTANCE" and very important, and not to rubber in on the conversation because it was "OFFICIAL POLICE BUSINESS!" She unplugged all the other connections to keep the line private on the Saugatuck end.

From the sound of the conversation, the coroner didn't seem too keen about driving over to Saugatuck on Sunday morning. Callie wasn't giving in. "This here is a murder investigation, so I don't care nothing about your plans. You can go to church some other time! They got evening services, so go then! You gotta get over here quick-like and do your job!" Callie hung up in a huff.

"Heard you and Frank Nitti were up all night drinking at the Big Pavilion?" Callie demanded of Doctor Horace's driver, Fred, when they got back to the *Aurora*.

"Yeah, I was with him, but I was drinking lemonade. No law against that," Fred answered. Horace smirked. Fred wouldn't have had anything stronger than lemonade, good Methodist fellow that he was.

"What time didja leave?"

"Must have been about one or so, when they were closing up."

"And then where'd you go?"

"I came back here and went to bed. What's this all about?"

"Nitti with you the whole time?"

"Pretty much. I went off to the gents a couple of times, but he was still at the table with the others when I got back. Leastwise, I didn't see him go anywhere. Why?

"Because I'm asking, that's why." Callie retorted. "You always hang around with gangsters?"

"No. I sat with him because I've seen him before, when he comes up to the doc's office. Thought I would be sociable. You know, good for business. Besides, he invited me over and it's not good business upsetting the likes of him."

"Oh, so Frank Nitti and his gang ARE good friends of the Balfours! I thought as much!" Callie looked at Horace and Theo, glaring at them in pure fury. "I'm getting the idea here. Pretty clear picture, to my way of thinking. Looks like my suspicions were right. I haven't got anything to hold you on, but see to it you don't leave town."

Fred looked confused, worried. "I'll tell you later, Fred. Just a lot of hot air from the chief," his boss whispered to him. He rolled his eyes for emphasis.

"All right, I've got questions for you two," Callie told Horace and Theo as they got back into the car.

"Like I said, I've got one for you, too. We'll go first." Horace said from the back seat. He let that sit for a few minutes until they got to City Hall.

"What have you learned from the widow?" Theo asked.

"Widow? What widow?" Callie asked.

"The parson's widow. The missus. Mrs. Smith. Don't tell me you forgot all about her?" Horace asked.

"Didn't know he was married," Callie said.

"So, you spent the whole night barking up the wrong tree with Frank Nitti and didn't even think to ask if the parson was married. Or had children. Or anything else that might have been helpful!"

"I'm only part-time around here, you know, and have a couple of fellows to help, and the mayor wants us to keep our costs down," Callie objected. "You should-a said something last night. That's evidence, and withholding evidence is a serious offense in my book!"

"So, you haven't talked with anyone out to Ox-Bow where Mrs. Smith was a student the past week. And you haven't checked inside the parsonage or vicarage or whatever they call it, either?" Horace snapped. "No, I didn't think so!"

Callie turned to a couple of young men who were lounging against a desk. "You two, make yourselves look useful and you get out to Ox-Bow and have a look-see on the road out there, too. You see anything suspicious, anything that isn't on the up and up, one of you stay there and keep watch, and the other one skedaddle back here to let me know. And if I'm not here, then find me." He pointed toward the door, "Go! And don't touch nothing!"

"And you two, don't even bother to sit down. Since you seem to have all the answers, you get yourselves up to the church and have a look around. They keep the key to the church house under the front mat. Well, that's probably where they keep it. Most folks do, if they even lock their house. Check the church first to make sure there isn't a body in there. Then do the house. You find anything, one of you stay there, and the other one get back here.

"And if you don't find nothing, then get back here quick like when you're done. I still got my questions for you two. Now get going and then get back. They hold their services at nine o'clock, and I want you back before then!" Callie ordered.

Horace and Theo didn't bother telling him that they had already inspected the church. "You get the feeling that maybe the chief hasn't had a murder investigation before?" Horace said drily. Theo snorted in agreement.

They went straight to the little parsonage. Just as Callie had told them, the key was under the mat at the front door. "Should have thought of that last night," Horace muttered in disgust.

It was a plain little bungalow, kitchen, living and dining room combined in the front, two bedrooms and an indoor bath in the back. A quick look at the kitchen made it clear that everything was in good order. If the padre had had dinner, or if he and his wife had eaten together, they'd cleaned up afterwards. Nothing left on the stove. Not much in the ice box, either.

The front room was just as clean. "Looks like they're either fastidious or else they were leaving today. Clean as anything," Theo said. "Almost like they weren't even here."

"Mrs. Walters said the wife was finished at Ox-Bow. Maybe they were going home right after services today," Horace reminded him. "Let's see the bedrooms."

The first one was made up, probably unused during the week. The second one was another story. Of the four rooms, it appeared to be the only one they used. The bed was made up, but rumpled, like someone had stretched out for a nap. Their clothes were in the wardrobe.

Theo looked carefully through the bureau drawers. His clothes. Her clothes. Underthings in the drawers. All neat and tidy. Nothing out of the ordinary. When he got over to the closet he knelt down to look at the floor and spotted a small suit case and pulled it out. He was about to open it when Horace said, "This is positively strange. Theo, take a look at this." He motioned at a small desk.

"What in the world?" Theo barely whispered. "Little religious paintings. Icons, aren't they? That's what they call them, I think. Icons. I didn't think an Episcopal priest would be caught dead worshipping a bunch of pictures. That doesn't make sense. More like the Catholics."

"Maybe he collected them somewhere?" Horace asked.

"Or Mrs. Smith did," Theo answered. "From what I saw of her, she didn't seem the type. Maybe she just liked having her trinkets around. Let's see what's in that grip I found in the closet."

Theo lifted the suitcase up on the bed and opened it. Both men were stunned to silence for a few moments. "What in the world is going on?" Theo whispered.

Horace picked up a bundle of money. "Russian. Roubles from before the Revolution. See, that's Nicholas II on the front. There's a fortune here."

"Was a fortune. It's worthless now. Just paper," Theo corrected him. He lifted out a packet to inspect. He fanned it through his fingers. "It might be worthless, but nice to dream about." He picked up another packet and froze. Beneath it was an ornate gold cross encrusted with rubies.

They stared at it for a few moments before Theo cautiously picked it up to inspect it more closely. Attached to the back were metal clips that held a string tie in place.

"Think it is real?" Horace asked.

"I don't know. It's heavy enough. Maybe. No, can't be. No one would be foolish enough to use real jewelry to make it into one of those funny looking ties. You ask me, they're positively ugly."

He passed it over to his brother to look at it. The two men were silent until Theo asked, "Now what?"

"First thing is to see if there are any more little surprises in there." They took out the bundles of money, fanning through them to see if something had been hidden. Both of them carefully ran their fingers lightly across the lining to see if there was something hidden behind it. Nothing. They put the money back in place. "What about that cross?" Theo asked.

"We'll hold on to it for a while." Horace slipped it into his pocket. "I got a feeling there is something important about this broach Let's see where they keep their suitcases. I'll check under the bed. You check the next room. And keep your eyes open for anything else. These two seem to be just full of surprises."

A few minutes later Theo returned with a suitcase in each hand. "Empty. Both of them. Should I put them back?"

"Yeah, probably that would be best," Horace said absently. "You know what's missing?"

"Aside from Mrs. Smith, and some way to explain all these loose ends? What?"

"Two things. Books and that wrapped up painting Mrs. Wilson gave him yesterday out to Ox-Bow. You ever know a minister that didn't have more books than he knew what to do with?"

"This one was just visiting. His library is probably to home," Theo countered.

"True. But there isn't a single book in here. Not a Prayer Book or a Bible. Nothing. Not even a magazine

"Unless they're out in his car already. If they were planning on leaving today, maybe he carried them out already. The car's still out on the street. We'll look on the way out. "There's something else missing, too," Horace said.

"What?"

"His sermon. Unless, it's over on the pulpit. Still, there's no paper, no pens. Nothing. It's curious, don't you think?" Horace asked.

What are we going to do with that grip with the money?" Theo asked.

"We'll take it with us for safe keeping. We can't leave it here in case someone comes snooping around. And if we take it to Callie he'll think there's a whole nest of Red spies holding a convention here and in cahoots with Nitti."

"And us. Don't forget, he thinks we're tight as thieves with Nitti as it is," Horace chuckled. "Wait until he sees us with all the Ruskie money!"

Horace put the valise in his cabin, locked the door, checked it again, and then joined Theo in the library. "Coffee, Mrs. Garwood?" he asked.

While she was out of the room, he opened the hidden compartment in the bookcase to return his pistol, and take out a veteran pipe and tobacco pouch.

"Regular little treasure chest you keep there," Theo teased. "Pistol, Scotch, and now a pipe and tobacco. I thought you had a personal war going on against tobacco."

"I have been working on a theory that copious amounts of caffeine and nicotine are beneficial when thinking," Horace answered.

"Best excuse I've heard in a long time."

The two men sat down at the library table, opposite each other. Horace pulled the strange cross out of his pocket and put it on the table next to the writing pad. "Let's see if we can figure out who's who," he said.

Theo waited, bored from inactivity, sometimes getting up to look at some of the books on the shelves, while his brother concentrated on writing his notes on a pad of paper. The only sounds were the scratching of his pen, and the occasion, slight clatter of the coffee cup on the saucer. The smoke from his pipe filled the room.

"Take a look at this, and see if you can figure out what's missing," Horace instructed him.

"That about covers it. Except for you and I being in with Nitti," Theo said, pushing the bad back across the table. "What did you come up with for an answer?"

They were interrupted by Mrs. Garwood with another carafe of coffee. She coughed at the thick atmosphere in the room. "I think I liked you better when you'd given up that smelly old pipe." She opened a window to air out the room.

"Send Gar to get some more tobacco," her employer instructed her. "If he doesn't know where to go, have him ask Phoebe. She'll know. And close that window!"

"On a Sunday morning? The only thing that's open on Sunday are church doors!"

"In this place? I'd say Saugatuck's pretty wide open. Just see what can be done, would you?"

"So, what's missing?" Horace asked again, nodding toward the paper on the desk.

"Nothing that I can see," Theo answered.

"All right, then you try diagramming it. Put Smith's name in the middle and draw a circle around it, and then everyone we've been in contact with the last day or so. Let's see where that gets us."

Theo worked on his assignment for a long ten minutes, then stopped, put down his pen, and looked up. "You know who you forgot? Mason. Doctor Mason," he barely whispered.

Horace stared at his brother, then blew the air out of his cheeks. "Mason."

"Makes sense, assuming he's the killer. He saw Mrs. Smith, and the last we saw of her she was talking towards his cabin. Maybe he hangs around and makes some excuse about driving back well after dark. He's missing. She's missing...."

"And, as a doctor, he'd know the one place to instantly kill someone is a blow to the cerebral cortex," Horace added. He didn't like the way this was going.

The two men sat in silence for a few moments, staring down at the list and then the diagram Doctor Theo had drawn. "You really think he did it? Maybe killed the padre and ran off with Mrs. Smith?" Theo finally asked.

"A love triangle? It makes more sense than pinning it on Nitti. A whole lot more," Theo said

"Yeah. Just don't like to think that someone we know had anything to do with it, that's all," Horace said glumly. "Besides, Mason mentioned something about a wife and children. He wouldn't do something like that if he was married and had a family."

Theo rolled his eyes. There were times when his brother was too other-worldly for his own good. Still, Mason was a real possibility. "Sort of hope it is Nitti and his boys. That'd take care of a lot of problems if they sent him to the chair," he said softly.

"Off to get you some tobacco," Gar said as he came into the library, forgetting, as usual, to knock on what he always felt was "his" boat. Phoebe was right behind him. He held out his hand for some money. "Say, pretty snazzy looking bolo tie fob you got there. Didn't think that would be your style."

"A what?" Theo asked.

"A bolo. Bolo tie. Like what those Argentine cowboys wear. Valentino wears one in the movies, too. Say, maybe you're going to take up movie-acting," Gar teased. "You dancing, maybe you're going to take up moving picture acting next."

"Argentine cowboys?" Theo asked.

"They wear them all the time. Argentine, Mexican, the whole bunch of them. Why, even William S. Hart wore one in the last picture show he made, too. You're gonna be right in style!"

"Gar, would you just get the tobacco, please! Thunderation!" Doctor Horace snapped at him.

"Aye-aye captain!" He turned to Phoebe and flashed a smile. "Avast me maties!" They left, leaving the door wide open behind them.

The brothers turned back to the papers on the desk, staring at them, hoping that something would catch their attention.

They were stumped.

CHAPTER FIVE

"Thank you for securing the evidence," Callie said when he arrived at the *Aurora* early that afternoon, and Doctor Horace turned the valise over to him. "It's not regular police procedures for a civilian to hold on to it, you know. Guess you thought you did the right thing. Maybe so...."

"We thought it was best. The fewer people who knew about it...." Theo said.

"Well, let's have a look-see at it," the chief said, putting it on the library table and opening it up. He stared for a moment or two, then let out a long whistle. "Lot of money in here. Lot of money."

"A lot of useless paper. It isn't worth anything anymore," Horace told him.

"What do you mean?" Callie asked.

"It's from imperial Russia. Time of the Czars. Lenin's running the country now and all that stuff is good for is starting a fire. Worthless," Theo explained.

"Just the same, someone's gonna want to get it back. Maybe you know that, but maybe they don't. Probably they knew Reverend Smith was carrying it and it was attempted robbery that ended up with murder.

"I ought to call the president of Fruitgrowers Bank and have him come down to open the vault to put it away for safe-keeping. No, that won't work, it's on a time lock, and he'll tell me I have to wait until Monday morning. Well, that's not going to work."

"Too bad," Horace said.

"Say, I got an idea. You fellows keep it here, locked up good and safe, and out of sight from the station. Now, if someone is missing that money they'll come down to the city hall to ask if we've seen it. Then we'll have our man! That's the ticket. You keep it here!" Callie said. "We got 'em trapped!"

Horace laughed. "Not a chance. They might have heard or seen us with that bag and they'd come here. I'm not playing cops and robbers. That bag leaves with you. Like you said, it's evidence, and you like to follow proper police procedures."

"Yeah, you might be right about that. Say, anyone tell you that we found Doc Mason's car? You heard that yet? Found it in a ditch just south of Pier Cove."

"And Mason? Theo asked, trying to not sound too interested.

"Found him knocked out cold a few yards away. Looks like he went off the road or something and hit his head."

"Alone, or someone with him?" Theo asked.

"All by his little lonesome," Callie said almost callously. "I suppose I ought to tell you, I sent young Ferguson from the funeral parlour to take the hearse down to get him....."

"I thought you said he was unconscious, not dead?" Doctor Horace countered.

"Well, I don't think he's dead. Ferguson and his father, well that'd be Ferguson and Son to be proper and formal like, has the furniture store and funeral home. They make a casket a man could be proud to be buried in, too. Pine, oak, whatever you want. They did one in bird's eye maple a couple of years ago that must have cost nearly a hundred dollars. Anyways, they use the hearse when we need an ambulance.

"He should be back here anytime now. I told him to bring the patient here."

"Here?" the Balfour brothers asked in union, with Horace adding a booming "Thunderation!" for good measure.

"Yup! Seeing as how you two are doctors and all, I figured this would be the best place for him. That way you two can take care of him and keep an eye on him all nice and safe and secure like. If I sent him up to the hospital in Holland I'd have to pay for a man to keep an eye on him. This way he gets medical care and can't make a run for it when he comes to. Well, if he comes to."

"No!" Horace said firmly.

"Absolutely not!" Theo added. "We're not cops."

"I don't see what the problem is. You got plenty of room here, you got a nice boat, you're both doctors, and you two and this boat aren't going nowheres until I say so. And that's final. You two are possible suspects and I'm not having you leave town. I'm doing you a favour taking that grip off your hands, so you're going to do one for me and keep Doc Mason.

"Besides, that's Ferguson pulling up now, and that seals the deal, as they say as far as I'm concerned."

Young Ferguson and Callie, plus Horace and Theo, carried the stretcher as carefully as they could up the gangplank, and then down to one of the cabins. Theo instructed them on carefully shifting Doctor Mason from the stretcher on to the bed.

"He's all yours now," Callie said with triumph. "Now, the moment he comes round, you get hold of me. Day or night. I got questions to ask him, and I might have more questions to ask the two of you. We still got a murder to solve and then figure out about that missing woman."

Horace was positive that Callie was cheerfully humming to himself when he and Ferguson left the cabin. "Thunderation!" he hissed.

Theo bent over Doctor Mason to examine him. "Better look at this, Horace. From the looks of it, we're going to have to amputate his left leg. Looks like the artery is badly crushed. What do you think? Does that look like gangrene to you?" He jabbed a straight pin into the man's leg.

Doctor Mason sat up in the bed. "Hey, there's no need to do that. Nothing wrong with my leg. I was just playing possum to see what was going on."

"And a good job of it, too. You fooled a couple of over-excited laymen, but that didn't work on us. I think you had better tell us what's going on," Horace said firmly.

Their patient pulled himself up the bed so he could rest against the cabin wall. "You got anything for a headache? I got clipped pretty good." He waited to tell his tale until after he'd swallowed several aspirin, washing them down with some tepid water.

"Your story," Horace reminded him.

Theo went to the door, opened it to make sure no one was in the passageway, then closed and locked it.

"Well, like I was saying, I got clipped pretty good." He pointed to the left side of his head. "I pulled out of here right after the fireworks show ended, figuring to drive down to Valpo and spend the night with an old friend from med school, then drive on home first thing in the morning.

"Anyway, I'm down near Pier Cove and I see some headlights coming up behind me, real fast. I figured they were in a hurry so I waved them to go ahead and pass me. I slowed down and got my right side on the shoulder, and let me tell you, down there, it isn't much of a shoulder. Anyways, they pulled up along side me like they were going to pass, and then ran me right off the road.

"I saw them pull up ahead and turn around, so I figured it had to be an accident, and they came back to help. Well, that's what I thought at first, anyway. They haul me out of the car and I guess I was a little shook up, cause they were yelling at me in what seemed like gibberish, and the next thing I know one of them hauls off and uses a big old fashioned horse pistol to knock me out cold. I went down as if the great Gentleman Jim Corbett himself had thrown the punch. I sort of came to a while later, and they were rummaging through the car and then drove off.

"I tried getting up but it was no good. I must have passed out again or something because the next thing I know it's daylight and someone's rolling me over. I played possum because I didn't know who it was – friend or foe. Learned that little trick during the war. And here I am! Except for a sore head, I'm ready to get back in the game, coach." He tried pulling himself up a bit higher on the bed and moaned. "Maybe not."

"Well, forget that. You heard the chief. He wants to haul you in for questioning, and you've got enough holes in that story to get you sent to the big house for a long stretch. He'll give you the third degree, for sure," Theo told him.

"Aside from a headache, anything else hurting?" Horace asked.

"All of me. I got banged up pretty good when I went off the road. Bounced around a lot, and up against the steering wheel a couple of times. Sore as anything, and aching. Nothing more serious than that. I'm banged up, for certain. That, and I'd like to sleep for a few weeks."

"No! Not a chance. Keep talking. Not a chance of that with a concussion. You're going to stay awake for a while longer. You ought to know that by now," Horace countered. "Look, Mason, last we saw of you, you were going out to Ox-Bow. So, tell us what happened from when you dropped us off here."

"Well, like I said, I went back out to my cabin. I had an idea for a painting I wanted to sketch out, so I worked on that for a while. I was just cleaning up and putting some things down in my hidey-hole when that Mrs. Smith came knocking on my door....."

"Hidey-hole? What's that?" Theo asked.

"I got this little trap door under the floor. It's under a rug under my easel. It's where I keep some of my supplies. You know, out of sight, out of mind, if the missus comes up with me, or when I'm gone if someone comes snooping around. Some of those paints and brushes are expensive."

"And I'll bet a bottle or two?" Theo smiled.

"Them, too." Doctor Mason flashed a smile.

"Anyway, she said she was wondering if I could give her a lift back into town. Which I did. She said she had some shopping to do so I dropped her off on the main drag and then went over to the Crow Bar for something to eat.

"Say, not to change the subject, but did you know Frank Nitti was in town? He was pretty lit up. Real tight, and I thought he was looking to cause a commotion, so I bought him a chop and spuds, thinking it might help sober him up a little. Not that it did much good. He staggered out of there like a drunken sailor. Said something about going to the dance."

"Yeah, we noticed. He stopped by here later on, three sheets to the wind," Horace said grimly.

"Well, I would have driven on home but I was a little lit up myself, and didn't want to drive like that. So, I laid off the hooch and hung around town to see the fireworks, and the rest I told you about already," Mason added.

"And you didn't see Mrs. Smith after you dropped her off?" Theo asked. "You're sure about that?"

"No, I didn't see her. Positive. Why? Something happen to her?" Doctor Mason asked.

"Not her. Her husband. He was murdered late last night. And she's nowhere to be found. Missing," Horace said flatly.

For a few moments Doctor Mason said nothing, taking it all in. "Say listen. If you're thinking I had anything to do with a murder or kidnapping or something, you got it all wrong, boys. Like I said, the last I saw of her is when she got out of my car by the drugstore. I didn't even hear about any of this until you told me just now!" Mason said quickly. "You boys are joshing me, aren't you?"

"No, we're on the level," Theo said. "The chief even tried putting the blame on Nitti, if you can believe it. And us. And Fred. The chief thinks we're all in on this. He's running in all directions and tripping over his own feet."

"Which is why we're going to keep you here for a while. Whether Theo and I believe you doesn't amount to much. It's what Callie thinks, and all he wants to do is solve a murder case in a hurry and play the hero which means he isn't thinking. Least not thinking straight. He's probably trying to get in the papers, him being the big crime-fighter and all. So, you're staying put for a while. Under lock and key, and with that curtain closed," Horace told him. "As long as Callie thinks you are unconscious he won't pester you, and that buys us a little time to figure things out."

Doctor Mason slumped down in the bed, thinking over all that he had just heard. "You two are pals," he barely whispered. "Just clear my name, would you? Get me off the hook."

"We're going to try to figure this out, and that's all I'm promising you. Assuming that you're telling the Gospel truth, it still isn't going to be easy. Mysterious road accident, getting clobbered on the side of the head by person or persons unknown, a murder and a missing woman..." Horace said quietly.

"You ever think maybe the missus killed her husband and ran off?" Mason asked.

"Yeah, that's crossed our minds more than a few times. The problem is, your problem, is that you were the last person known to have seen her. And from what I've seen of Callie, he'll either think you did it together, or that she did it and you got her out of town. If he can't find the murderer he'll try pinning you for being an accessory to a murder," Horace told him.

"Balsam juice!" Mason said.

"Balsam juice? What's that mean?" Theo asked.

"Balsam juice. Yeah. The wife doesn't like me cussing around the children so I just say balsam juice. No one knows what it means and it sounds dirty. Picked it up from a patient who's a writer for the railroads. You ever hear of a fellow named Sam Campbell? Nice fellow."

"Glad you got your sense of humour, because I got a feeling you're going to need it," Theo said.

"Look Mason, we're going to leave you for a while. And no sleeping. I mean it. Not in your shape. Not for a few more hours. We're going to lock the door. Now, keep quiet. And you hear the key in the lock, you pretend to be unconscious, understand? I got a feeling that Callie will want to have a look at you before long. And keep that curtain pulled. The cabin is right on the deck. You don't want anyone looking in." Horace told him.

"Got it. Loud and clear, " Mason said. "What are you two going to do?

"That's a good question right now. Truth be told, I don't have an answer," Horace said.

"And I've got a question for you," Theo said once they were back on deck. "Just what are we supposed to do now that we're hiding a murder suspect? We're getting in a little deep, don't you think?"

"Like I told Mason, that's a good question, and I don't have an answer for that one, either," Horace said.

"We ought to do something," Theo sighed.

"Well, let's look at what we got. Callie and a lot of others are back out to the school looking around. I had Fred drive Harriet, Mrs. Walters that is, and Phoebe out there. Gar and his missus have the day off, same as always. That leaves you and Clarice and me.

"Theo, you and that Trix fellow have known each other for years. What do you say to looking him up and the two of you going for a wander around town and see if you can find out anything. Folks will talk to a musician. See if he's heard anything. Or, that Ollie fellow.

"Listen, those two fellows are from Illinois, Chicago area, aren't they? So is Mason. It's a long shot, but maybe they heard something or ran into someone that said something. You know what those jazz musicians are like. Sound like a plan?

"About as good as any, even if it is a long shot," Theo said. "What about you?"

"Staying here and taking care of Mason," Horace said.

"Mason should be okay, but if you say so."

"Yes, Mason might be all right – so long as Chief Callie doesn't come calling. And there's another thing. Remember, someone ran

Mason off the road and then came back to rough him up and hit him with a big pistol. Maybe that's the way it happened. Maybe they were a bunch of hotheads. Or, ..."

Theo interrupted, "Or, maybe they're still looking for him. And Callie wasn't exactly the soul of discretion bringing him here. I see what you mean.

"Say, you'll be all right on your own, won't you? Maybe you ought to keep that pistol handy...."

It was a very tired group who later slouched and slumped in the deck chairs on the *Aurora*. When Gar offered to walk over to the Corner Shop for a pail of ice crème, even Phoebe was too tired to go with him. "Not much to show for a long day," Clarice said softly. She let out a long yawn. "None for me, but the rest of you go ahead." Gar reluctantly got up to walk into town.

"I know, we hiked back and forth and crosswise and back again out to the school and didn't find a thing," Mrs Walters said. She watched as Phoebe suddenly got up. "Where are you going, dear?" she asked.

"Up to the wheelhouse to practice my Morris Code," the girl said.

"Morse Code," her mother corrected her.

"Morse Code," she answered.

"Why are you doing that, Phoebe?" Clarice asked.

"Because Janie Bird told me that girls couldn't learn Morse Code, and I said I could. I'll show her! Gar set up something called a practice key for me. I already know some of it."

"What about ice crème when Mr. Garwood gets back?" her mother asked.

"I've GOT to practice," she said firmly.

"That girl's got pluck," Horace said approvingly. "But you were saying you found nothing."

"Nothing, for which I am truly thankful."

"And we didn't have much luck, either," Theo yawned. "Say, I did learn something, but it hasn't got anything to do with the murder and missing woman. Horace, you got those musicians all wrong. I know you don't care much for their music, but I ran into their leader, that Ollie Anderson. Good thing you're sitting down when you hear this. They're all Boy Scouts! Can you beat that?"

"They're too old to be Boy Scouts," Horace countered.

"Yeah, well they are now. Sure. But Ollie got them together in the summer of 1917, to help raise money for War Bonds. You know who they played for? John Sousa, himself. They must be good because they raised so much money Sousa pinned a medal on him. They've been playing ever since, all over the Midwest. Boy Scouts. Clean cut fellows as they come!"

"Can we stay on the subject? Reverend Smith is dead and his wife is missing so let's not get sidetracked," Horace said firmly. "Theo, what did you and Clarice get out of Trix and his fellows?"

"Nothing. They'd heard about the padre, of course, but nothing more than that. Well, just the same rumours we've been hearing all day. You know where they first heard the news? When they were at the Methodist Church this morning. Tells you the sort of fellows they are doesn't it? Just shows they're good fellows." He yawned loudly. Horace glared at him in disgust.

Gar arrived with the ice crème just as Callie pulled up in his truck. "How's my suspect doing? You bring him around yet?" he shouted from the sidewalk.

"Our patient is still unconscious," Horace told him. "He had a pretty bad knock on the head."

"Can't you docs do something to snap him out of it, or is that what the ice crème is for? Wouldn't mind some if you got extra."

"No. And you might as well know that when he does start coming round, if he comes round, which might not happen at all, we're going to watch him very carefully. If he starts thrashing around we may have to induce a coma to keep him quiet until the swelling goes down. The important thing right now is to keep him quiet and let nature take its course," Horace said firmly, leaning on the rails.

"That so? Well, I still want to talk with him," Callie demanded.

"Look, if you try rushing someone with a brain injury it could create more problems. That is, unless you want to be investigating two murders, of which you'll be the cause of one of them."

"That serious?" the chief asked.

"That serious!" Horace replied, nodding his head for emphasis.

"Well, you see to it I'm informed as soon as he's awake. Got it?"

Horace ignored him and sat down for a few seconds. He got up again. "Checking on our patient," he said to no one in particular, and went down to Mason's cabin.

By the time he came back on deck Harriet and Phoebe had left. "They're tired. Besides, Harriet has to be out at Ox-Bow in the morning to teach," Clarice said. "Ice crème is in the ice box if you want some."

"What's Phoebe doing tomorrow?" Horace asked. His question surprised his brother, and even himself. It wasn't usual for him to take that much interest in someone.

"Gar said she could work on her Morse code in the morning. Anyway, it's getting late. We're turning in." Theo stood up and helped Clarice to her feet.

"All right. I'm going to read for a few minutes. Care to join me in the library?" Horace asked.

Theo shook his head. "Not tonight. We're turning in."

"All right. Sure you don't want some ice crème before it's all gone?

"Don't be up too late. You could use some sleep yourself," Theo cautioned.

CHAPTER SIX

Doctor Horace was, if anything, a man of routine and habit. He was up early and dressed, and then out for his morning walk. A fast pace. Ninety steps to the minute, same as a Sousa quick march, just as he had marched on the parade grounds during the war. Back straight, shoulders back, eyes forward. In the early morning it was how he came fully awake, brushing away the cobwebs after a restless night. He always walked the half mile to work, summer or winter. A walk later in the day, two walks, some days, to stave off being drowsy. Only when he was ready to go home for the night would he telephone Fred to bring the car.

To his comfort, the streets were all but empty. A few shop keepers were sweeping the sidewalks in front of their shops, all of whom said, "Good morning" or "Nice day." The cafes were open, of course, for the early morning regulars. All locals And a few delivery wagons and trucks were unloading. Horace snorted in disgust. Whoever had laid out the city had forgotten to include alleys. He didn't approve the practice of unloading merchandise and carrying it through the front door. "Dead common," he muttered.

He was through with Saugatuck. Murder or no murder, now that Gar said he would finish the repairs by the end of the day, he was eager to go. One way or another, he'd tell Callie that he was leaving. He'd spent enough time in the Great Saugatuck Waiting Room. He'd come up with a reasonable story, little more than a partial truth, that he was needed back at the hospital and was taking the train home. A medical emergency. Big important operation, life and death. Gar could get the *Aurora* home on his own.

He was walking down Water Street when he saw Phoebe, a few blocks ahead of him, going toward his boat. Doctor Horace slowed down. "Well, maybe tomorrow."

Another few hours with that girl wasn't the worst way to spend time.

He and Theo ate a light breakfast. Clarice was still sleeping. Phoebe had eaten at home and was already up in the wheel house practicing her Morse Code. She had explained she wanted to learn all the letters, and then the numbers.

"Any plans for what we do next?" Theo asked.

"Mondays have always been your day for rounds. That means Mason is your patient this morning. See if you can get him to say anything more. Or catch him in a lie or something. Anything." Horace knew that his brother had a far better bedside manner.

"What about you?" Theo asked.

"I want to find out where this Reverend Smith came from. Clergymen don't just pop up out of nowhere. He had to get his degree from somewhere and get ordained by a bishop somewheres. Someone had to make arrangements to get him here. So, someone up at All Saints' must have made arrangements."

"Any idea who that might be?" Theo asked.

"No, but the best source of information has got to be that telephone operator. Ever know one that didn't know everything that was going on in town? Telephone operators and barbers and I haven't seen a barber pole. Best and quickest source of information, even if it isn't the most reliable." Horace said. He pulled out his pocket watch. "By now someone ought to be there. I'll be back as soon as I can."

"You might find out from Phoebe, too," Theo countered.

"I'll be back," Horace replied. Even if Phoebe would happen to know, a conversation with the telephone operator might be more helpful. Once Horace got her talking he might learn much more than just a name or two.

Doctor Horace was gone for over an hour. "How's Mason?" he asked, sliding into his favorite chair.

"Doing well, and bored. He wanted something to read so I loaned him a book from your library. Trust you were finished with the Sherlock Holmes. You've read it often enough you ought to have it memorized by now. I'm half surprised you haven't worn the words off the page just from reading it so much. And told him to hide it under the covers when he wasn't reading it. And you? What did you find out?"

"Nothing useful. A fellow named Barbour pretty much runs everything up there at the church from his office in Chicago – when he isn't up here. So, I called down to the city, and guess what? He's on vacation for another week. His secretary said she didn't know anything about what goes on up to All Saints.

"The operator told me that the bishop has his office up at the cathedral in Grand Rapids. St Mark's. I called up there. Take one wild guess? Not only is it his day off, but he's off on vacation for the month. And his secretary said that I should talk to the senior warden!"

"That's the run around for you. Then again, I'd hate for anyone to try to get hold of us, you know?" Theo said. "Say, at least you found a Barbour if not a barber pole."

Horace ignored the pun. "I called the hospital to let them know where we are. Stuck in the waiting room! Thuderation!" he bellowed.

The two men sat in silence.

"Now, I did find out that there is a small college up the road in Holland. Hope College, it's called, and the operator said it's tied in with the Dutch Reformers," Horace finally said.

"And how's that going to help?"

"The only thing left I can think of is to find out about this cross that we found. It just doesn't make sense that an Episcopal minister would have all those icons and all that Russian money, and this thing. Probably it's Russian, too, but I don't know. Maybe if we can get a handle on that we'll make some progress," Horace said.

"What do you have in mind?"

"I don't know for certain. But after lunch, I'm going to have Fred drive us up to Holland to see if we can find out anything about this thing. Colleges have libraries, and libraries have librarians, and librarians are full of information." He flashed a wan smile.

"All right, drop me off here," Horace said when Fred pulled up to the front of the college. "Pick me up in two hours."

"What do you want us to do while we're cooling our heels?" Theo asked.

"You two scout around town. See if you can find an armoury, Legion Hall, or something like that, and talk to someone. See if you can figure something out. And if you don't have any luck, find the Masonic Lodge. Maybe the secretary is there. I don't know why he should be. Seems that everyone else is off on a vacation or working. Two hours, Fred, no more, remember!" He got out of the car, leaving Theo and his driver.

"You got any ideas, Fred?" Theo asked.

He put the car in gear. "Not yet. We'll drive around a bit and get a lay of the land. Maybe something will show itself." They had spotted the Armoury, stopped for Theo to get out, but the doors were locked. He turned to drive down the main business street, going slowly, as they looked at both sides of the street. For the most part, small shops and businesses. It didn't look very promising.

"There we are!" Fred said, quickly pulling the car into a vacant parking space. "Follow my lead, sir!"

He jumped out of the car, then hurried over to a barber shop, just as the owner was closing. "Come back in an hour, would you?" the man asked. "Lunch time," he added, pointing to the sign in the front window.

Fred chuckled. "Bit late for lunch, isn't it?"

The barber looked at his wrist watch. "Time for my lunch. I stay open over the noon hour when fellows can take a break, then take mine around one."

"Say! Wait a minute! Hold on! I know you! You and I were in basic training back in '17. I can't always remember a name, but I sure don't forget a face." He thrust out his right hand to shake with the barber. "You remember your old pal, Fred, don't you?"

"Yeah, you look familiar. Yeah, sure! Say! Glad you made it home all right!"

"Well, you did okay yourself. I heard you got a field promotion. That right?"

"Yeah, and when the lieutenant went west, the captain promoted me. And you? Where'd you get sent after training?" he asked Fred.

"France. Just in time for Hindenburg's big push. Hospital orderly. Say, meet my colonel. After we got back I signed on with him and I'm his driver now. Nice steady job."

"How do you do?" Theo said formally, sticking out his right hand. "No need to salute. We're all civilians now."

"Please to meet you, sir."

"Say listen, ah, ah....." Fred began.

"Charlie, Charlie Dudowlowski," the barber said.

"Yeah, that's right. How I could forget a name like Dudowlowski is beyond me. Anyway, Charlie, the colonel and me was thinking about having something to eat. You got a good place close by?"

Charlie snorted. "Do I ever. Place called Warm Friends Tavern. New place, and the food is best anywheres around. Down in the basement. I'm just heading there. Come on with me."

Fred and Theo followed their new friend down the street for a block or so, entered the building, and went down in the basement. The tavern was nearly empty now that the lunch crowd had finished and gone back to work. There were a couple of fellows playing cribbage at one table, and the cook leaning against the counter.

"Anything on the menu is good. And in case you're thirsty, they got ... well, you know what I mean?"

Fred gave him a big smile. "Nothing beats a cold beer on a hot afternoon. One for you, too, Colonel?" Theo smiled and nodded.

They ordered, and then Charlie got up to go down the hall. It gave Theo a moment to ask Fred how he knew that a barber he had just met got a field promotion.

"His watch. Officers all had wrist watches, especially in the infantry."

"I'm impressed," Theo said.

"Don't be. It's a cheap Waltham."

"I meant, I'm impressed with you knowing that."

"So, you two were in France. Me? I got sent up to Russia."

"Ah, knock it off. Russia was out of the war before we got into it. You pulling my leg?" Fred asked.

"Nah, I'm serious. Sure, Russia got knocked out of the war, but they had all those supplies we'd sent them, and a lot of stuff the Brits sent them, and Germany wanted them, and the Kaiser and that fellow Lenin were cozying up to each other. So, they sent us up to guard the stuff before they could make off with it. You know what those Bolshies are like - steal anything that wasn't nailed down. And after a while the big-wigs figured we ought to take on the whole Bolo army. Me, I was in the 313th Engineers," Charlie finished his beer in two gulps, and held it up for a refill. "You boys buying?"

"Of course. I never heard about any of this," Theo said.

"It'll set you back a quarter, but I guess you can afford it, having a chauffeur and all," Charlie said. "So, like I was saying, they wanted us to take on the whole Bolo army. Lenin, Trotsky, all them Russians."

"Bolo? Who were they?" Fred asked.

"Bolos? Bolsheviks. Bolos, that's what we called them. You know, Reds. Murderous cut throats. You think you had it rough behind the lines in France? Let me tell you. We got Bolos shooting at us. We got mosquitoes big as a zeppelin . We got cooties gnawing away at us. Bad food. Cold food. No food. And winter. They got winter up there. Right near the Arctic Circle, you know. Some days the sun was up for an hour and then dark again. Couple of boys, we found them frozen stiff, dead. And then we got the White Russians shooting at us, same as the Bolos. Leastwise, that's what they said they were."

"Never heard about any of this," Fred said, his beer still untouched.

"Course not. We got our tail feathers kicked but good. Course you never got to hear about it. The army didn't want to talk about it. Not a bit. They probably didn't want us to talk about it much, neither. Few of us still get together, though. You know, remember the bad old days."

Theo signalled the waiter to bring their guest another beer.

"Thanks!" Charlie said, hoisting his mug. "To the Polar Bears!"

"To the Polar Bears!" Fred and Theo answered. Fred pretended to take a sip. He noticed the cribbage players look up from their cards.

"Jimmy over there, now, me and him were buddies. Translators. See, I speak a little Ruskie, and I taught him some of their lingo. Safer than being up the line. Him, too, but not so much. So, they made us question the prisoners, things like that. What we didn't know, we made up.

"Hey, Jimmy! Get yourself over here and show them that fancy medal some grand duke or some-such gave you," Charlie shouted to the fellow behind the bar. Jimmy limped over, with Charlie explaining how he lost his big toe on his right foot to frostbite.

"Jimmy, show him your medal that grand duke pinned on you!"

The barman reached in his pocket to pull out a medallion. Theo whistled in appreciation - and to mask his surprise. It was identical to the one he had found in the suitcase.

"That there, boys, is a genuine official Medal of Saint Stanislaw! Turn it over Jimmy and show them the backside."

He passed it around the table. "See how we fixed it up? Made it into a tie holder, you know for those western type ties Wyatt Earp and Doc Holliday wore. It's our way of sticking together. Sort of our secret password. Polar Bears over the bolos. Pretty good joke, huh? Polar Bears over the bolos, get it?" Charlie asked loudly.

"But I got the last laugh on the big shots for the way they treated us. You know what I did? Well, I'll tell you what I did. I voted for that Eugene Debs in the last election! Voted Socialist. That'll show them. That's what I think of them in Washington!"

Jimmy put his hand on Charlie's shoulder. "Take it easy, friend. Talk like that aint much good for business. Yours or mine. Keep it down, would you? You don't know who's listening and talk like that's dangerous."

"Yeah, sure thing, Jimmy," Charlie said.

Fred interrupted, "Sir, if you are still planning on going up to Grand Haven, we ought to be back on the road."

Theo nodded in agreement. He looked at Charlie and Jimmy. "It has been a pleasure meeting you both. Perhaps our paths will cross again." Charlie remained seated and made a half-effort at saluting him.

Theo paid for another beer for the barber.

"You're full of surprises, Fred," Theo said when they got back on the street. "First, finding that barber and convincing him that you two were old army buddies. And then not drinking any beer."

"Thank you. Sheer good luck, that's all. And I didn't have any beer because I took the pledge back when Billy Sunday was in town. Shook hands and everything," Fred answered. "Took the pledge and joined the Methodist Church."

"A man of convictions," he said in appreciation.

Doctor Horace was sitting on the front steps of the college administration building, waiting. "Learn anything?" he asked his brother and Fred once he was in the car.

"Plenty," Theo answered.

"Me, too. First thing I learned is that this place is run by the Calvinists and they don't have much good to say about anything Catholic. But the librarian told me that this is a cross of Saint Stanislaus, some Russian Orthodox holy man. That didn't tell me much."

"That's what we got, too, except they pronounced it 'Stanislaw'" Theo answered. "Only a whole lot more than just a name. Apparently, the Czar awarded them before 1917. The ones afterwards, when Lenin was taking over, came from the White Russians loyal to the old regime. And they're made out of red glass. Worthless. We met up with a fellow who got one from the Whites."

"Not this one," Horace said.

"You're sure about this one of ours being genuine?" Theo asked.

"Positive. I had time to walk down to a jewelry store. It's definitely genuine. Worth a fortune. Now, the funny thing is, there are a lot of false ones right around here...."

"We know. That's what we found out, too," Theo began to explain.

The three men continued to compare notes all the way back to Saugatuck.

"And all of that means we are more confused now than when we started! Thunderation!" Horace exploded from his favourite chair in the library. He slammed his fist against the leather arm for extra emphasis.

"None of it is logical," Theo agreed. "Two sets of these medals. A real set and the phony ones. Reverend Smith's is genuine ruby; those fellows in Holland have glass. And yet, whoever killed him didn't take the money or the medal. If it had been his wife, surely she would have known about the medal and taken it before she disappeared. But she didn't. Doesn't make sense to me."

"And if those icons were valuable, they were left right out in plain sight, too," Horace reminded his brother. "I don't know if they are genuine or just copies. None of this makes any sense. Period!" He was in a foul mood. "You know what I can't figure out is what they're up to. It's almost like they've got some secret society going on."

"You don't suppose they turned on our Reverend Mr. Smith for some reason, do you? Maybe he gave away their secrets or let the cat out of the bag? Something like that?" Theo asked. "Or knew too much."

The two men sat in silence.

Horace's mood did not improve when Clarice came into the library with a pitcher of lemonade and cookies. "I'm surprised Phoebe isn't with you," he said.

"No. She worked on her Morse Code for a couple of hours and then I think she got worried about her mother being up at Ox-Bow or something with a murderer around. You know how children and their imaginations are. Truth be told, I think she was the one who was scared and wanted her mother," Clarice explained. "Anyway, I'd baked some cookies, so I suggested she take a bag of them with her to share with Mrs. Walters."

"How did she get there?" Theo asked.

"Probably the same way she always does. She took the chain ferry across the river and walked up the trail," Clarice said, filling Horace's glass.

"That doesn't make good sense, either. She's worried about her mother being up at the art camp where there are all these people around. There's a killer on the loose. And she goes up there by herself. You sure she didn't want someone to go with her?" Horace asked.

"Very sure. I offered, but she said she'd rather go by herself."

"Strange."

Theo laughed. It's not strange at all. A young girl, a bag full of fresh-baked oatmeal cookies. Of course she wanted to be on her own. And I'll bet her mother never saw those cookies, either!"

"Meanwhile, Nurse Balfour, how is our patient?" Horace asked.

There had been no change.

Callie paid a visit right before dinner. "I heard you boys went up to Holland. Business, or just a good excuse to get away for a cold beer? Folks in Holland generally come down here to do their drinking so their neighbors don't know about it. You could have had a cold one over to the Crow Bar."

"Why, captain, you know that's against the law. Prohibition, remember?" Horace countered. "We were there on medical business."

"Too bad. Saugatuck is where all the action is. Think we got a lead on what happened." He started coming up the gangplank and sat down on one of the deck chairs. "If it pans out, I guess I'll have this case solved and wrapped up in no time.

"See, I got a report from a couple of college boys that had come up here from Chicago. Guess they got themselves pretty tanked up and didn't feel all that good yesterday or they would have been in to see me. They still looked a bit worse for wear today, if you want my opinion. Must have been bathtub gin. The cheap stuff. Maybe they brought it with them. We don't allow bootlegging here," he said with a smile.

"Anyways, they said they were down along the river bank with some flapper types to see the fireworks. I'm pretty sure they were out-of-town girls, office type or secretaries up here on a lark. They said they saw a woman come down the street carrying a brown paper bag and walk straight into the water. Just walked in like she was on dry ground! Can you beat that?"

"That's terrible! Why didn't they stop her?" Clarice asked.

"They thought she was going in for a swim or something. Must have thought that, though I doubt they were doing much straight thinking," Callie answered.

"You think it was Mrs. Smith?" Horace asked.

"They didn't get a good look at her. Leastwise, they can't remember what she looks like. Like I said, they were pretty tight. But it fits the description of her.

"So, the way I see it, she killed him and then gets all remorseful like and drowns herself." Callie seemed rather proud of himself. "Murder and suicide."

"I take it you're still looking for the body?" Theo asked. "You would have said if you'd found it, right?"

"Yup! I got some of the fellows with boats going up and down the shoreline to see if they can find the body. Course, we might not get that lucky. Current's pretty fast, and if she didn't get snagged on something she could be halfways to Wisconsin by now."

"What about this paper bag she was carrying?" Horace asked.

"I figure she was carrying the murder weapon. See, when you been in the policing business for a while you can figure out murder and suicide. They go together, specially if it is man and wife. The gun's probably down in the muck and mud, so we'll have to dredge for it."

"Good work, chief. So, that more or less lets Doctor Mason off the hook," Theo asked.

"Maybe it does and maybe it doesn't. I still want to question him about all of this. And about his car accident, too, if it really was a car accident. He isn't up and about yet, I take it."

"There's some movement, but that's about it. He floats in and out. These things can take time. Like we said before, rush a patient along and you can sometimes end up with a death," Horace said flatly.

"That serious, huh?" the policeman asked.

"That serious," Horace affirmed, watching as a dejected Callie got back in his car.

"What do you think? Think there's something to what he said, or just a smoke barrage?" Theo asked.

His brother snorted. "With him, who knows? Could be. Maybe not. Who knows? Anyway, we're not taking any chances just yet. Sure is full of himself, isn't he?"

"Well, Clarice wants to go for a stroll in town. Thought I'd go with her, unless you need me here. Or, you want to come?" Theo asked.

"No. I want to see if I can find the weak point in this," Horace said firmly. "I'll be in the library."

Theo knew better than to ask a second time. His brother had that far away look in his eyes that said he was working on a theory. He was just as certain that Horace wanted to be on the boat when Phoebe returned.

CHAPTER SEVEN

Doctor Horace retreated into his library and closed the door. He spent a couple of minutes spreading out his notes and the charts he had drawn, covering the table. Almost involuntarily he reached for his pipe, filled and lit it. 'Somewhere the answer is staring me in the face. Thunderation!' Where is it?" he said to himself. He stared, shifted pages and notes around, reviewing everything.

Over the years he'd learned to marshal his thoughts, make notes, and then create strong medical papers. Short, terse sentences. No filler. Make a point, illustrate it with case examples, conclude it. It had been hard at first. But this, trying to sort out the human heart and emotions and all of their physical responses, was impossible. Utterly impossible.

He burned his way through a box of matches. More matches than tobacco, as he tried making sense of it. Something was either right in front of him, or it was the missing factor. Or worse - missing factors. Plural.

"Ahoy the *Aurora*! Permission to come aboard?" he heard a voice from the sidewalk below. It was Harriet. To his surprise, she was alone.

He waved her up the gangplank, surprising both of them when he reached out to take her hand. "Where's Phoebe?" he asked.

"One of her friends invited her to a sleepover. Well, to be honest, I called on Nell's mother and suggested it, and she agreed. I thought with all the girl has been through with that Mrs. Smith and all, that she needed a break. Something that would take her mind off of it," she said.

"Very wise of you. She's old for her age, but still...."

"Anyway, I ran into your brother and Mrs. Balfour in town and they said you were here on the boat. So, I stopped by the corner shop and bought a boat-warming gift." She held up a small paper bag. "Boat warming, or maybe it's boat-cooling. Anyway, it's ice crème. That is, if it's a good time...."

"The perfect time for ice crème is any time!" Doctor Horace smiled.

"It's rocky road - vanilla with chunks of chocolate. I liked the name and thought it might make a peace offering for our rocky start. I think I was pretty rough on you," she said, looking down.

"I think we were both a little out of sorts. But I do like the pun. It's the sign of a sharp mind," he laughed. The deck was beastly hot under the late afternoon sun, and he led her back into the library.

"The atmosphere is a bit thick in here," he apologized.

"I rather like it. Phoebe's grandfather smoked a pipe," she said absently, looking at the papers on the desk. "I'm interrupting you." She didn't see him flinch.

"Glad for the distraction. I'm still trying to make sense of the murder. And I'm not making any progress on it. I'll be right back. Let's enjoy this before the children come. I'll take this out to the galley and get some spoons and bowls."

"Children?" she asked.

"My brother and his wife, and no telling what strays they might find along the way," he teased.

"You just did it again," Harriet told him.

"Did what?"

"You smiled and laughed. Two smiles, one laugh. You really can smile when you put your mind to it. It does make your face look much more, well, handsome." Harriet blushed, knowing her remark made her sound as if she was flirting. She only wanted to offer a well-deserved compliment. Nothing more.

Doctor Horace took his time in the galley, pausing for a moment to look at his reflection off the window. He flashed a smile at himself, thought he looked silly, and returned to the library. Harriet was looking at the notes on his table.

"Sorry. I shouldn't pry," she apologized.

"Nothing very secretive. Just my method of trying to make some sense of it all," he said. They sat down opposite each other in the thick leather chairs.

"Here's a thought to add to the confusion," Harriet said. "What if our Reverend Mr. Smith wasn't really a vicar?"

"The vicar wasn't a vicar?" Horace asked. "What leads you to think that?"

"Well, he said he was a vicar, and he had the right clothes for it. But what if he wasn't really one?

"You mean, an imposter?" Horace asked.

"Well, yes. I mean, we have visiting priests here every summer, but we generally get a letter from Mr. Barbour or the bishop or someone letting us know. We didn't know anything about this Reverend Smith until he got here. That's a bit strange," Harriet said slowly between nibbles at the ice crème.

"The letter could have been lost in the mail, you know," Horace countered. "I tried reaching this Mr. Barbour by telephone, but his secretary said he was out of town. But anyway, he couldn't just turn up here and move in. What if there were other arrangements or something?"

"I know. But the other strange thing is that Mrs. Smith didn't register with Ox-Bow like the others. She just turned up late on Sunday afternoon and presented herself. Everyone else applies and registers months or weeks in advance, either through the office down in Chicago or up here."

"How do you know?" Horace asked.

"Because I was in the office when she came in. She said that her husband was the supply clergy at All Saints and that she wanted to paint at Ox-Bow for the week. Just like that. And then she pulled out her purse and said she'd pay cash."

"A bit audacious, wasn't she?" Horace asked.

"More than a little audacious. She had all her supplies with her like she wasn't going to take no for an answer," Harried answered.

"Or, unconventional. Or, maybe she didn't know the way you do things there. So, how did she get in so easily?"

"Money. We're always running tight, so when she pulled out cash, we weren't going to object too much. And, we had the space for one more artist. We can usually fit one or two more in most classes. Even the popular instructors will squeeze in someone more."

"Except, I remember you saying she wasn't much of an artist....." Horace said slowly.

"She wasn't. She played at it, not worked at it."

"I think there's your answer. She was on a bit of a lark, and that's it."

"If he was who he said he was, then yes." Harriet answered. "Maybe she was just having a laugh at our expense, mocking us. That's what angers me more than anything else."

"Or, if she was who she said she was. Or, for that matter, if they were both really who they said they were. We start going down this path and we'll get nowhere. Before long we'll decide they are a couple of novelists working on a book, or Hollywood film writers coming up with ideas for a new script, or, or, or, well, why not spies?" Horace was exasperated.

"Spies? Around Saugatuck? There's nothing here to spy on. No secrets. Well, of course there are, but nothing out of the ordinary."

"No. No there isn't. Or, you can wonder if she's some sort of black widow that goes around marrying someone and then killing him for the money or the insurance. And if you start following that line of reasoning you'll get off on a wild goose chase. Best leave that sort of thing to your police chief."

They sat in silence, finishing their ice crème, their spoons chattering against the china as they sought out the last taste.

"You're probably right, you know," Harriet finally said. She paused, then burst out laughing. "You know, if it wasn't such serious business, it would almost be fun if Callie did think they were spies! He'd be running around like a chicken with its head cut off."

Her comment made him laugh out loud. "Say, now that would be fun, and we're not going to do it. He's over his head as it is. All he wants to do is solve this murder and get on the front cover of the Police Gazette. He'd pin the murder of Cock Robin on Nitti or Doctor Mason or anyone else if he thought it would work."

"I know," she said sadly. "So, do you really think it is murder and suicide? That's so sad."

"I'm beginning to think it is. It is the only thing that makes sense. Simple, straight forward murder, remorse, and suicide. It really does make sense," he said sadly.

"It doesn't make sense!" Harriet said quickly.

"Unfortunately, most of the time murder does make sense. Not always, but most of the time. It makes perfectly good sense to the murderer at the time. Sometimes, even the victim. Figuring out why they killed someone is the tough part. If it really is murder and suicide, that's the end of it right there." He looked at her, and she turned away, staring out the window, lost in thought. He knew something was troubling her. For some reason a shiver ran down his spine, and he was certain it had nothing to do with the coolness of the ice crème.

"No, not always," she barely whispered. "What about Doctor Mason, then?"

"I think it was little more than coincidence. He said he was driving back home late on Saturday. I think he either got shoved off the road or went off on his own. You know, lost control of his car. I don't think he had anything to do with it Anyway, we'll know more when he comes to." Horace said, careful to keep his patient's recovery a secret, even from Harriet.

"I s'pose that's good, in a way. I can see your point. I mean, all of the young people up at the Presbyterian Camp, the students at Ox Bow, all the people in town. If it was a murder, or a murder and kidnapping, it could have been any of them, just as well as Doctor Mason," Harriet said almost bleakly.

"I don't really know the man. Theo knows him better. But I'm just as happy it isn't anyone I know, even casually."

They sat for a while in the library, noticing the shadows lengthen as the sun finally slid behind Mount Baldhead. It was quiet, and something they both discovered they appreciated. Just sitting in silence was comfortable.

Harriet sighed. "I should be getting home."

"I thought Phoebe was with a friend for a sleep-over," Horace said.

She laughed. "She is. And if she gets homesick she'll expect to find me at home. Phoebe is at the age where one minute she is all grown up and the next, still a little girl. She's at that age." Harriet laughed again. "The other evening she told me she could tuck herself into bed. Ten minutes later she's asking for a bedtime story. So, I'll be home in case she needs me."

Horace stared into space, silent, knowing that if he had not worked so many late evenings he might have seen that in his own children. Too late now.

She stood up to leave, and Horace walked her to the gangplank. "It's been a lovely few hours," she said, staring into his eyes.

"It has," he repeated quietly. He reached for her hand to give it a squeeze, but froze, unable to make the gesture. She paused and smiled at him, and walked down to the sidewalk.

Horace watched as she walked down the street. "Well," he said softly. He returned to the library to turn off the lights and pull shut the door.

"Strangest thing in the world," Gar told his wife as they had their breakfast the next morning. "I told the boss that the boiler is all patched up and we're going to fire her up. Told him it would take the day to get up some steam and then see how everything's holding together. And I told him we could probably leave tomorrow or the next day at the latest. And you know what he told me? You have any idea?"

"What?" she asked.

"He looked at me, real quiet-like, and just said, 'that's fine.' Nothing more. Just that it was fine. I don't know that he's feeling all that well. Maybe he's come down with something," Gar said.

"And you made that diagnosis all by yourself, did you? He tells you that, and you can't figure out what ails him? Well, I'll tell you what he's come down with. The man's fallen hard for that Walters woman! You couldn't see it or figure it out!"

"At his age? It's you that's daft, woman! Either that or you've been into the cooking sherry!" Gar chortled.

"At his age. Yes, indeed. At his age! And you'd better be feeling the same way about me, and at your age, too!" she laughed.

"Well, what do you know. The boss has a heart after all."

"And he'll never forgive himself if he lets that girl slip away. He'll not get many more chances like that one."

"Old girl, I'm telling you that you're wrong! You'll see. You read too much. Put's ideas in your head."

Horace put down the two-day-old newspaper when Theo sat down at the table. "I'm beginning to think that maybe Callie is right after all, much as I hate to admit it. Mrs. Smith killed her husband and then killed herself. Simple as that. And as for our friend Mason, he went off the road or was forced off the road, and that's that. Just a couple of unrelated events. Simple, and to the point."

"And simple is usually best," Theo sighed. "A bit disappointing, isn't it? Just plain old murder and suicide. But you're probably right."

"Well, it was diverting while it lasted, but let's face it, we're surgeons not detectives. Not even rank amateur detectives. Anyway, it's about time to go back to being doctors. Gar tells me the boat ought to be ready by tomorrow, the day after at the latest. I've already told Mason that we're leaving and he's got to face the music with Callie."

"How did he take it?" Theo asked.

Horace shrugged his shoulders in uncertainty. "About all he did was repeat the story he told from the beginning. He said he'd been trying to remember anything else, but there just wasn't anything."

"You told the chief yet that we're leaving, or about Mason?"

"No. I'll walk over to City Hall this morning and tell him. I suspect he'll be over here on the double so he can talk with Mason."

"And that's the end of all of that," Theo said softly.

"Not quite. I want Mason kept out of sight," Horace whispered, leaning closer to his brother.

"Why?"

"If, and I'm just saying 'if' someone tried to run Mason off the road, and if, and I'm still just saying 'if,' it was for a reason, then it's best if no one knows where he is. Just being cautious, that's all," Horace said.

"And when you leave, then what?"

"He's going with us. We'll tell Callie he needs to go to a proper hospital down to Chicago. Look, we're going right through Chicago, and that's where you'll get off. You are Clarice, if you're taking the train back home. Stay on if you like, more than fine with me, you know that, but we're still going through Chicago. We'll let Mason off there and from then on he's on his own."

"He knows this?"

"All I told him is that he could ride down to Chicago with us on the boat. No point worrying the man over a maybe or a could be or a big nothing."

"So, you still DO think....?" Theo started to ask.

"No. No I don't. But that doesn't mean throwing caution to the wind, either," Horace retorted. Theo nodded in agreement.

"You got a notion in your head. I saw it before Clarice and I went out last evening," Theo said, paving the way for his brother to talk. He pulled up a chair to join him for breakfast.

"What?" Horace asked.

"It's something you said earlier that made me think this through from a different angle. It's those Polar Bears. They all went up to Russia, and they all got those medals from the government. But our Reverend Mr. Smith's medal is real. The rest of them are cheap imitation red glass. You said it was like they were some sort of secret organization.

"What if, and it's pure speculation, but what if Smith had told secrets and the Holland fellows wanted to silence him? Or what if Smith came here because someone was talking too much and he was supposed to silence him, only they got to him first?"

Theo looked at him, his eyebrows shooting up. "That may not be such a far-fetched idea. This Charlie the barber that we met up with, he was getting loud after a couple of beers and the barkeep told him to pipe down because someone might hear him. He said he'd voted for Debs in the election, if you can believe it!"

"That's something, isn't it? A little dissension in the ranks, maybe?" Horace thought about it for a moment, "Ah, let's forget about this whole thing. It's not our job to figure it out. Anyway, I'm ready to go home."

"One more thing to think about, Horace," his brother said. "I'll bet you haven't told Phoebe and her mother that you're planning on leaving.

"No, not yet."

"And you're toying with the idea of just slipping away quietly without saying a word, aren't you? I know you are, so don't deny it. It's going to be hard enough on the girl when you leave, but it's unforgiveable to just leave without saying goodbye. I mean it. You tell her yourself or Clarice will have plenty to say about it, and no mistake about that!"

"I'm sure the girl is old enough to know that we can't stay here forever," Horace said.

"Just the same, she's going to take it hard. So is her mother."

Horace knew his brother was right, but he still didn't want to have that conversation. There had already been too many 'good-byes' in his life. It didn't make it any easier. For a few moments he mentally ran through the roll call. His parents, his wife, his son, colleagues, school mates, patients. They all hurt at the time; they still hurt now. He had more dead friends than live ones. It didn't make this one any easier. He'd have to tell her. It was the right thing to do.

"Incoming!" Theo hissed, then nodded to the street down below. "Chief Callie." The officer didn't wait for an invitation, much less stand on ceremony, but came up the gang plank.

"We were just talking about you," Horace said, standing up to shake hands. "Theo and I came to the same conclusion as you. Murder and suicide. Looks like you figured it out right from the start. Good work, chief."

The chief smiled. "I'll feel a lot better when we find the body. If we find the body. I still got the boys out looking along the shoreline to see if it got snagged. And, to watch for birds."

"What's bird watching got to do with this?" Theo asked.

"Old lawman's trick. I'll let you in on a professional secret, cause I know you won't go telling everyone. You watch for birds. Turkey buzzards, crows, scavenger birds. That type, not your little song birds. If you see them circling around that usually means there's something dead down below. A body. In this case, a human body." He nodded triumphantly.

"You can trust us. We won't tell a soul," Theo said solemnly.

"Now, what I came here for was to see if Doc Mason is sitting up and taking nourishment yet. It's been a long time. Even if he isn't the murder suspect, and I don't think he is, I still need to get the details about his auto wreck. I'm as patient as the next man, but like I said, it's been long enough."

"Well, Callie, this must be your lucky day. Mason is coming out of the coma. He's not up to eating solids yet, but give him a couple of hours and get some water into him, and by this afternoon you can talk to him as long as you like. Or need," Horace told him.

The chief clapped his hands together in pure glee.

Callie had no more than left the *Aurora* when Mrs. Garwood knocked on the door. "Doctor Horace, I hear tell from my man that we're going to be sailing in a day or so, and I was thinking about that little girl, Phoebe. And besides that, I overheard you talking because I was listening. Your brother is right, she's going to be pretty sad. But I had an idea while I was washing up. Why don't we make it a celebration the night before. Gar could take the *Aurora* out for a little late evening cruise. Say, maybe down to that Oval Beach place, just in time to watch the sunset. And Doctor Horace, Doctor Theo bought those sky rockets. You could light them off and make it special. I'll bake a cake and everything. It would give her something special to remember. You, too."

He thought about it for half a minute, then nodded his head. "We'll take that under consideration." She started back to the galley, and he called after her. "Thank you, Mrs. Garwood. It IS a good idea. Thank you."

Theo and the Garwoods were right, of course. Phoebe did take the news badly. Tears welled up in her eyes, even if she tried to be very grown up about it. "But I'll miss you, Doctor Horace!" she almost wailed.

"Yes, and I'm going to miss you very much, too. That's why we're going to have a special celebration. A cruise down the river and out to the lake, and I did promise you fireworks, remember? Our own personal, private show!"

She did remember, and her face brightened.

"Will you promise me something else, Doctor Horace?" she asked.

"What would you like?"

"Well, tomorrow will you drive me out to Ox-Bow so we can pick up Mother? You do know how to drive a car, don't you?"

"Of course, I do. I've been driving since I got my first car, and before that, I drove a pair of chestnut horses and a carriage. Only now I've gone from two horses to eighty!" he laughed.

"You've got eighty horses!" she asked in surprise.

"Yes dear, only they're all under the hood. An eighty horsepower straight eight engine."

"Just you and me until we pick up Mother?"

"Just you and me!" He surprised himself and reached out to give her a hug. "Now, don't you think you ought to go up to the wheel house and practice your Morse Code for a while?"

Doctor Horace watched her go up the steps. "I'll be back," he told Mrs. Garwood. "Fish for dinner, I hope."

She watched him as he walked down the street, and breathed a sigh of disappointment. He was wearing his straw boater straight on. "The old fool. Cutting and running again." She muttered to herself.

CHAPTER EIGHT

Phoebe had enjoyed her car ride with Doctor Horace out to the art school. At first she had wanted to sit in the back seat, pretending to be a very grown-up lady. That lasted about one minute. She could do that later. She wanted to sit next to her friend in the front seat, and this might be her one and only chance; certainly her last chance.

When they got to the school, she carefully, and ever so politely, instructed him to back in next to the Old Inn. "Mother may want to put something in the trunk," she explained. He unlatched it for her, and then let her lead him by the hand down to the water's edge. To his relief, there were no figure models posing for artists. They found a wooden park bench and sat down to stare out into the water.

For a long time they sat in silence, each lost in their thoughts. "I'll be back," Phoebe said in a whisper, then darted off toward the Old Inn. When she returned a few minutes later she had a couple of slices of bread.

"Hungry? Don't spoil your dinner," Doctor Horace cautioned.

"Not for us. We can feed the turtles over at that dock!" she told him. She pulled him by his hand up to his feet, once again leading him.

"Watch!" she said. She ripped off a piece of bread and tossed it onto the water. Almost instantly a snapping turtle surfaced to gobble the bread. They could see several more just beneath the surface. For the next few minutes they took turns, each throwing a piece of bread, sometimes far from the dock, to watch the turtles and a few small carp. Then a much larger carp swam in from the deep waters, and the others scurried away.

"You two look like you're having fun," a voice said behind them. Phoebe and Horace knew it was Harriet. "I'm done for the day, so any time you're ready to leave....."

The three of them drove back to the *Aurora*. Fred was waiting for them, ready to back the car onto the boat. "Thought if we were taking the *Aurora* out for a test run tonight, we ought to go fully loaded," he said.

"Good thinking. Thank you, Fred," Doctor Horace said, handing him the keys. "Don't worry. I didn't hit anything. Not a scratch on MY car," he teased.

The doctor didn't see Fred wink at Phoebe.

Mrs. Garwood had decided they would have a buffet dinner on the deck. The serving table would be in the library, making more room for everyone to sit together. As they neared the end of their meal Doctor Horace slowly looked around the table, looking at each of his guests. If Phoebe had looked more closely, she would have said that he looked very sad. He felt sad. And old.

"I'm delighted we could all share this meal together. As you know, our plans are to leave tomorrow, so we're going to make this a special evening for all of us," their host said. "And, I especially want to thank Miss Walters and her mother for such a warm welcome in their town; and to each of you for making it a very memorable time. Mason, I think you went well beyond the call of duty providing the entertainment." Everyone laughed.

"And you'll all be happy to know that Callie isn't sending me up the river to the big house!" he interrupted.

"So, after we've had our dinner and helped Mrs. Garwood clean up, we'll cast off and go down the Mighty Kalamazoo River. Fred says there's no wind so we'll go out on the lake down to Pier Cove and come back. If we time it right, we'll drop the anchor off the Oval Beach, and as soon as the sun sets, Miss Phoebe will FINALLY have her own private fireworks show. That sound good to everyone?" he asked.

Everyone cheered and agreed to the plan.

"It sounds LOUD to me!" Phoebe giggled.

"Say, Horace, I've got to run to the drugstore for a minute. If you're lighting off those sky rockets we'll need some punk sticks," Theo told him.

"You just now thought of that?"

"Better now than when we're ready to light them. I'll be back double quick march. Straight there; straight back. Promise."

"Go, then. And no stopping to talk to anyone, and no diversions. Get there and get back! Thunderation!"

Horace followed Gar down to the engine room to look at the pressure gauges. "She looks good. Nice and steady, and all the joints are holding tight, pump working. I've given her a clean bill of health. Fine shape for her age. She's good to go as soon as we get up another ten pounds. Shouldn't take more than twenty minutes, tops."

"All right, and let's not push it. This is a test cruise, not a race," Horace cautioned. "Your stoker knows he's supposed to keep checking the gauges?"

"I told him, shovel then check, shovel then check. Don't you worry none about Royce. He'll do a fine job. If she works the way she should, what say we let him come up on deck when we light off them rockets?" Gar asked.

Doctor Horace didn't give an answer. They'd come to that question once they got to the Oval Beach.

Horace waited on deck, leaning against the rail, eager to once again get in motion. He smiled, Theo was coming along the sidewalk, but then he looked again. Nitti was with him. Right behind him. Something about that didn't seem quite right. The gangster was walking too close behind his brother.

"Gar, Mason, get ready to cast off. Mason, take the bow line. Fred, as soon as Doctor Theo is aboard, crank up the gang plank and we'll be on our way," he commanded. Despite his concern for what was unfolding, his voice was calm and steady.

"Hello, Horace ol' buddy," Nitti smirked. "Beginning to look like you were about to take off, and me not having a chance to say my good-byes to you. I didn't figure that was right and proper etiquette for a couple of upstanding gents and your girlies, so when I saw your brother here, I said to myself I ought to come along."

"What's going on, Nitti?" Horace asked. Theo was looking rather pale and shaky, and Nitti continued to stand right behind him. Close.

"I figured you folks would like to give me a boat ride down towards South Haven way. Well, let's just go to South Haven, what do you say? No need to say anything other than 'yes.'"

"We're not going that far. Just out to the mouth of the river and back," Horace said evenly.

"Sure, sure you are. But I think we'll go down to South Haven. Change in plans, right, Theo?"

"You'll have to talk to my brother. It's his boat. But Horace, I think it might be a real good idea," Theo said, a few beads of perspiration were forming on his forehead. He lifted both of his hands up just slightly.

"Well, that is certainly something we should take under consideration. It'll take half an hour to get out to the lake, the better part of an hour just to get down to South Haven. There won't be much to see by then. It'll be dark before we get there. Might be more enjoyable just to stick with our original plans," Horace said slowly.

"I think a long cruise would be a lot more healthy," Nitti sneered. "What about you, Theo? Don't you think South Haven would be better, a little more healthy like?" Theo flinched suddenly and nodded in agreement.

Capone's enforcer hadn't noticed Mrs. Garwood watching from the galley door. Nor had he seen her slip back inside to get a cast iron frying pan. And he certainly had not seen her slip out the door and behind him. She held the handle with both hands and slammed it against the right side of his head. He dropped to the deck. Mrs. Garwood looked at her skillet to be sure she hadn't dented it.

"Thunderation! What the blazes is going on? Never mind. You can tell me later. Get him into the library now! Fast!" Horace barked. Mrs Garwood, Theo, and Horace pulled Nitti into the library. Horace loosened his collar to check his pulse. "Still alive, thank goodness." He stood up and demanded, "What in thunderation is going on?"

"I was buying some cigars at the drug store because they didn't have any punk, and Nitti was standing next to me. We were talking and I said we were taking the boat out. Well, he followed me out the door and stuck a gun in my back soon as we were on the sidewalk."

"A gun? A gun? Did you see a gun?" Horace demanded. "Well, did you? Do you see one now? No!"

"No, but I felt it. And I wasn't in any position to hold a debate with him," Theo said. "Not just then, I wasn't."

Horace was furious and repeating himself. "Theo, do you see a gun because I sure don't see a gun! Mrs. Garwood, do you see a gun? No. No you don't see a gun because there is no gun. How long have you been a doctor that you can't tell the difference between a gun barrel and a finger?" Horace opened Nitti's coat. "There's his gun! Still in his holster! Thunderation!"

"Well..... I, ah...." Theo sputtered. "I haven't had much experience in having guns shoved into my back."

"Never mind. We better move fast before his pals show up, and then we'll really see some guns!" Horace shouted.

Hearing the shouting, Gar and Harriet tried to come through the library door at the same time, got jammed, backed up and tried again.

"Is he dead?" Harriet asked, her hands over her mouth.

"No, just knocked out cold by our Mrs. Garwood and her frying pan!"

"You okay?" Gar asked his wife.

"I think I'm going to faint," she whispered. Harriet and Gar nearly tripped over each other when they rushed to steady her.

"Never mind her, she'll be all right! Gar, get up to the wheel house and get us out of here. Pull out nice and slow. No wake. We don't want to draw attention. And make sure we've cast off before you start. I don't want to take the dock with us.. Slow and easy. Natural. Go!" He watched as Gar hurried out of the library and scrambled up the stairs to the wheel house. The captain blew the horn, and the engines were chugged to life. He didn't need to be told to go slowly. There wasn't quite enough pressure.

"Harriet, go in the galley. Find a big mixing bowl and fill it with warm water," Horace told her.

"Warm water?"

"Warm water. A bowl of warm water. Not hot, not cold, warm. Luke warm. Tepid. Stat!" He turned to his brother, "Help me get him up on the chesterfield."

Harriet returned with the bowl of water. "What's this for?" she asked Horace.

"Old fraternity boy trick. A little diversion that just might save our hides. Put his left hand into the water and hold it there." Horace instructed. He felt through Nitti's pockets until he found a flask, opened it, and poured some whiskey onto him. A little on his face, the rest down his clothes, and then put the bottle into his right hand.

"Oh dear!" Harriet gasped, looking at a growing wet patch on his pants.

"Good," Horace said. "All right, you can take that bowl back to the galley."

"But he's..."

"Yes, I know. When he comes to he'll think he had an accident from too much booze. Some of your education is severely lacking, young lady. You would have known this if you'd hung around frat houses." Horace said, smiling for the first time. "Now, take that back, find Clarice, and bring her in here."

"That's Frank Nitti," Clarice said in alarm. "Is he dead?"

"We noticed, and no, he's not dead. And if we survive this, Theo has a wonderful tale to tell you. Later. All right, in my bag there is a bottle of ether and some gauze. Think you still remember how to administer it like you did when you were my nurse?"

"I haven't done it for thirty years!" she gasped.

"The procedure hasn't changed. Gauze over his mouth, if he starts coming to, a couple of drops. No more. We want him sleeping, not dead. All I want you to do is keep him under. Just barely."

Horace leaned over the gangster and removed the pistol from his shoulder holster.

"He carries another piece on his right leg," Theo said.

"Do you think this might be a good time to help out a little and take it?" Horace asked with sarcasm. "Clarice, sing out if you have any trouble."

"Gar, anything coming up behind us?" Horace shouted.

"No. Nothing! Doc, go down to the engine room and get a reading off the pressure gauge, would you? Should be somewhere in the green."

Horace dashed down to the engine room, then up again. "Green. Low end. That good?"

"Sure is good. Right where I want her."

They slowly sailed out of town, beginning to relax. "Let's wave. Make it look natural, like we're having fun," Horace said when they were approaching some men fishing from the dock. They did, and the wave was returned. The passengers on the *Aurora* were breathing more easily. So far, it didn't appear that any of Nitti's friends were coming up behind them, and since there wasn't a road out to the breakwater, they had a renewed sense of safety.

"Just look natural," Horace reminded them. "We're just going out on a pleasure cruise."

"Steamboat round the bend!" Gar shouted from the wheel house. "She's the North America. We gotta make way for her." He pulled on the signal to let the stoker know they were at full stop. Very carefully he let the momentum of the river carry them forward, and slid the *Aurora* as far to starboard as he could, then signalled again, quarter reverse, to bring her to a dead stop in the water; then he signalled for a full stop. They were tight against the shore, with some poplar branches brushing against the upper deck.

Almost instinctively, several of them grabbed hold of the branches as if they could steady the *Aurora* from sideswiping the passenger ship.

The captains of the two ships exchanged greetings with their whistles, and the passengers waved down to the small group on the *Aurora*. "Too bad they missed the show," Theo said.

"Oh, do keep quiet!" Horace hissed at him through his smile. "We're not out of this jam you got us into!"

There was little more than a bare twelve inches between the two boats as they passed. Once the North America was clear Gar signalled full forward, and the engines came to life again. The two big paddlewheels beat against the water, and they picked up speed.

Gar put two fingers in his mouth and whistled down to Horace and Theo, then pointed to a young man in a small boat coming out of the lagoon. He went past in a hurry, picking up speed. "Fisherman," Gar shouted. "Saw his poles. Perch must be running down near Pier Cove, off the rocks in the shallows." Horace waved in acknowledgement. That seemed safe enough, and the man in the boat hadn't appeared very interested in the *Aurora*. Horace didn't think he had even looked in their direction.

The delay while the North America passed them meant that it was getting closer to sunset by the time they reached the mouth of the river. Lake Michigan was spread out before them, smooth and glassy. For a few minutes Doctor Horace stood at the bow. Under normal circumstances he would have been swept away by the sight, but this was not a normal night. Far from it. He pulled out his pipe and lit it, watching the smoke blow toward the stern. Theo knew to keep his distance and keep quiet while his brother was thinking.

Horace knocked the ashes and dottle out of his pipe, then went up to the wheel house. "All right, Gar, slow her down when we get to the Oval, and go slowly until we get down to the Douglas Beach. Nice and slow, so everyone can see us, right up until the sun goes down. And let's get the lights on so we stand out. Understood? I want everyone to see us until we get past Douglas. Then we'll go down to Pier Cove. I want to pull in there so we can let off our ah, passenger."

"I hope so. She might have silted in with that storm," the captain said, thinking about the landing there. His charts were up to date, but a storm could change everything in a matter of hours.

"I know. We'll have to take our chances. Now Gar, by any thin chance do you or the missus happen to have a bottle of beer or two with you?" Horace asked.

"Why, that's against the law!" Gar said, teasing. "Prohibition, you know!"

"Yes, I know. President Coolidge told me that just after he poured me a sidecar," Horace answered.

"You had drinks with the President?" Gar asked.

"Yes, and do you have any beer? That's what I want to know!"

"I suspect that if you went down to the galley Mrs. Garwood might have some, but its strictly for cooking purposes only. She uses it for fish batter and pancakes, that's all. We wouldn't want to get caught breaking the law, you know."

"Good. There is some beer in the galley since she certainly didn't use it to batter fish!"

"Yes, sir. And if you're thirsty, then you're more than welcome to it seeing as how you paid for it when you got the grocery bill."

"You and my brother and your wife are just full of surprises to-night," Horace said firmly.

"Why, that's just part of our charm!" Gar teased, then quickly added, "Sir!" He turned his attention to the wheel, watching for other boats and snags in the water.

"All right, Theo. You and Phoebe go get those sky rockets and bring them up here. When we get close to the Oval Beach, I want you to set them up on the shore side. Take your time doing it, so everyone can see. Keep the girl busy, and keep her out of the library." Horace commanded.

"What about her mother?"

"See if she wants to lend a hand with the rockets. Take her mind off things. I don't think she should go into the library, either."

"When are we going to set them off?" Theo asked.

"Soon as we drop Nitti off at the pier. He stinks to heaven of that rotgut whiskey Capone sells. And I got a couple of bottles of beer Mrs. Gar keeps on hand. Between getting clobbered on the head and the booze and his wet pants, he'll think he was on the bender of all benders. Oh, first go check on how Clarice is doing, would you?"

"Just did. Her patient is out for the long count. Your Mrs Garwood's got the swing of Babe Ruth!"

"Well, tell her not to get carried away. Nitti probably had a few bumps of whiskey before he decided to shanghai you. He doesn't need a second one from her."

Harriet had recovered from her shock of seeing Nitti wet himself, and she came across the deck with a full head of steam. "What is going on?" she demanded. "What is that, that, that killer, doing here? You are friends after all, aren't you? Admit it and tell the truth."

"The simple fact is that Nitti got the drop on Theo at the drug store. I don't know if he was up to mischief or needed to get out of town in a hurry. Probably the latter. I think he wanted to get out of Saugatuck because he didn't have his goons with him. That's why. I don't know the reason, and right now I don't care and it doesn't matter. And Mrs. Garwood got the drop on Nitti with her frying pan. Now we're in a jam, and we're going to razzle-dazzle him a little, drop him off at Pier Cove and leave him.

"This is not what I had planned. Trust me!" Horace answered calmly. "It's the truth! I promise!" For some reason he spit into his right hand and slammed his left fist into it. Harriet stared at him in shock. "Phoebe taught me," Horace smiled.

She was not placated, and she certainly didn't find it amusing as she stormed off toward the stern to calm down.

The *Aurora* passed the Oval Beach to the cheers of a few late evening swimmers who were waiting for the sunset, then the Presbyterian Camp, and the Douglas Beach. Gar blew the whistle to return their greetings, and they cheered again.

The sun was just resting on the horizon, still shining brightly across the lake in Wisconsin. Horace pulled out his pocket watch. "So far, so good." Another half hour and they would be rid of Nitti and could relax. He would forgive Theo later, and apologize. Maybe.

"Boss, better get up here!" Gar shouted from the wheel house.

He pointed several hundred yards out to the west. "That's the boat what passed us in the channel, only there are four of them now, and I don't see any fishing poles. Something doesn't feel right. Gives me the willies up and down my spine. Sorta reminds me about the time the Huns tried slipping up on us." He handed the field glasses to Doctor Horace.

"Doesn't look right, either. Looks to me like they're up to something. We got to watch out. Keep an eye on them." Horace said quietly. He watched their outboard motor churn up some water, and they turned toward the *Aurora*. The boat circled wide, coming straight toward the bow, then at the last moment, veered off to come along side, splashing water onto the deck.

"Think they're drunk or something?" Horace asked.

The two men watched as the launch went past, circled out into the water, and made a second run at them. They zoomed past again, two of the men in the boat shouting and shaking their fists at the *Aurora*, another one held up a pistol to fire off a shot.

"What in thunderation are they up to?" Horace asked. "Starboard. Hard a starboard. Take us out into deeper water!"

"Deeper?"

"Yes! Do it. If they think they're going to run us aground they got another thought coming!" Gar pulled hard on the wheel, turning the *Aurora* to the west. "Four hundred yards, then straighten her out!"

The launch made a third pass, this time the man with the pistol took direct aim at the wheel house, putting a slug in the wood over their heads.

"What's going on? Harriet shouted up from the deck.

"Get down, woman, and stay down! And get Phoebe down flat on the deck and keep her there!" Horace bellowed. Harriet froze for a second, then dropped down on the wood. She scurried toward Phoebe on her hands and knees, and pulled her down, wrapping an arm over the girl to protect her and keep her from jumping up.

Theo came out of the library, wanting to know what was going on. "Someone shooting at us?" he asked.

"You think? Yes, someone's shooting at us!"

"Who'd you set off this time to get them so angry?" Theo asked, still not knowing the situation to take it seriously.

"Get back in there. Turn off the lights and get Clarice on the floor. Nitti, too!"

Theo's eyes widened, realizing that they were in danger. "What's going on?" he shouted back at his brother.

"No idea. Get those lights off and keep down!" Doctor Horace watched as the small boat made a wide circle out into the lake and then paused. It looked like they were making up their next plan of attack. And that gave him a few moments to think. He watched the lights in the library go dark.

"Gar, let's drop these windows. Break them out if you have to! And throw me that megaphone!" Horace ordered.

The captain tossed the megaphone at him first, then opened the windows. Glass wouldn't stop a bullet, but it would shatter and cut up anyone inside. The side windows opened easily and he locked them in place on the ceiling. The front window was stuck tight and had to be broken. Gar used a wooden stool to smash them, sending shards of glass onto the catwalk in front of the wheel house.

"Theo, you buy anything but those rockets?" Horace shouted through the megaphone.

"Yeah, a whole bunch of lady fingers. For the girl to play with," his brother answered.

"Go get them and bring them here!"

"Mason! Mason, there's a spot light on the stern. Go. Now, don't turn it on until I give the order. Wait until I tell you. We'll wait until they're close enough to blind them. Get going! And keep down! When I give the signal, turn them on, and then right back off again.

He watched as his guest crawled on his hands and knees toward the rear of the *Aurora*.

"Incoming!" Gar shouted.

The lake was nearly navy blue dark, but they could see and hear the boat coming their way. "Down everyone!" Horace shouted. He reached into his pocket and pulled out Nitti's ankle gun. It was nothing more than a six shot thirty-two calibre revolver, a toy except at close range. Or a lucky shot. A shot from a moving boat at a moving boat would be a very lucky shot.

Horace waited until the launch got closer, then stood up and fired off two rounds in their general direction. He was certain he hadn't hit anything, probably not come even close, but at least they knew the *Aurora* was going to play hardball with them. They weren't going to raise the white flag, and they certainly weren't going to go down without a fight.

"You're shooting a GUN at them!" Harriet wailed in protest.

"That's the general idea! They're shooting at us. Now keep down!"

They listened as the boat made a tight turn to pull away. Horace hoped they would have something to think about before they returned.

"Who? Who's shooting at us?" Harriet wailed.

"Right now, I don't know, and I don't know why. Pirates for all I know, not that it matters!"

"Pirates?" Phoebe asked. "Real honest to goodness pirates with the Jolly Roger and everything? Gosh!" Her mother shushed her.

"Mason, you ready on that light?" Horace shouted.

"Ready!"

"Wait for my order!"

Phoebe got up on her hands and knees. "What can I do?" she asked.

Doctor Horace was about to tell her to stay down. "You think you can send a message on the radio telegraph? It's the real McCoy this time, not for practice."

"Yes. Well, I think so."

"All right, stay right there. When I tell you, you run up those stairs to the wheel house, and you get down on the floor and stay put. Gar will get the radio telegraph down to you." He turned his attention to the captain. "Hard starboard, ninety degrees, straight west. When Phoebe gets up there, straighten her out again."

They waited for the ship to turn, putting the cabin between the girl and the launch. "Now!" Horace told her. "Remember, stay down!" Phoebe ran up the stairs, holding on to both railings, and dropped down to the wheel house floor.

"Here you go, girl. Put this on. I wore it all during the war." He handed her the metal helmet and helped her put the leather strap under her chin. It was far too big for her, and the strap dangled useless at her throat.

"Ready to send!" she shouted.

"All right. Send SOS South Haven Coast Guard. Repeat it. SOS South Haven Coast Guard. Then tell them the *Aurora* being shot at. Have you got all that, girl?" Doctor Horace asked.

"I think so. I've got it! Gar can help me." She paused for a moment. "Sending!"

"You want to make yourself useful, woman?" he asked Harriet.

"Yes!"

"Go down to the engine room. First, check the gauge, the big one near the boiler, and make sure it is still in the green. Then find any old nuts, bolts, ball bearings, anything like that and get them up here. Alright go. They're still far enough out. Move!" She crawled across the deck to the door leading to the boiler room. From the bowels of the ship she shouted, "Green. Right in the middle. It's green!"

That was good news. They weren't in danger of an explosion. At least not yet.

"Fred, you and Theo go up front to that signal cannon....."

"We haven't got any cannon balls or shot for it," Fred interrupted. "It's a signal cannon!"

"I know that. You know that. They don't know that! Load it, and when they come back close, let 'em have it."

"Bout all we'll do is scare them to death!" Fred objected.

"Well, you got any better ideas?" Horace roared at him. "Theo. Give me one of those cigars! And let's have those lady fingers."

"Any response from South Haven?" he shouted up to Phoebe.

"Not yet!"

"Send it again. Give them twenty seconds. Count nice and slow. Then repeat it again. And stay calm. Keep doing it until they answer! Have Gar make sure the radio's on the right frequency!"

"What's the right frequency?" Phoebe asked.

"Never mind. Gar knows!"

It was now fully dark. The advantage was still with the men in the launch. They could see the outline of the *Aurora* against the house lights and bonfires along the shore. "Zig zag, Gar. Irregular zig zag. And keep us well away from shore. We don't want to get hung up. Deep water!

"Battle stations everyone! Prepare to repel boarders!" Horace shouted through the megaphone. "Here they come. Wait for them. Wait for them. A little longer...."

"Fred, fire!" Fred touched one of Theo's cigars to the fuse, and they crawled away from the cannon. They could see the sparks as it burned down. A pause. The cannon barked, lifting itself off the deck, in a cloud of smoke and halo of sparks, and the boom echoed off the sand dunes on the shore.

"That got the Boche on the run!" Fred cackled. Theo didn't bother to tell him that the war had been over for a decade. "Turned on a dime and high tailed it all the way home to Berlin!"

"Phoebe! Report!"

"Nothing yet. No! No! They're answering. They're answering. They heard us! Loud and clear! Now what?"

"Send this message - *Aurora* near Pier Cove southbound. Someone shooting at us. Shots fired. Come PDQ! You got that? *Aurora* near Pier Cove southbound. Shots fired. Come PDQ!"

"Got it!" She was on her hands and knees, her helmet sliding down over her face, but she managed a salute.

"Good girl. Knew you could do it." Doctor Horace turned to Harriet. "Take that stuff up to Fred and Theo. They'll know what to do, and then get down here to help me. Wait until Gar turns the boat." They waited, standing close to each other. "You scared?" he asked.

"Yes! You?" she answered.

"Right down to my shoe laces. All right, go. Up and back, quick!" Horace watched as she darted across the deck and up the stairs to the small deck on the bow.

As soon as Harriet was down on the deck Horace ordered the *Aurora* made another sharp turn. "Now what?"

Horace pulled out the cigar, bit off the end, and spit it on the deck, reaching with his other hand for a box of matches.

"That's disgusting," Harriet fussed.

"This isn't the time for Paris Manners." He lit the cigar and took several long drags on it until the end had a nice glow on it. Now, crawl over there and light one of those rockets. The moment you do, get out of the way. And don't drop the cigar. You'll have to puff on it to keep it going. Fire when ready!"

He watched as she scooted across the deck, found the fuse with her fingers in the dark, lit it, and scurried out of the way. Harriet gagged and coughed from the cigar. The rocket arched through the sky, leaving a trail of sparks, seemingly paused at the zenith, and then erupted with a thunderclap that echoed off the bluffs behind them.

"Good one!" Horace shouted at her. He had no idea if it would be the least bit of help.

"South Haven Coast Guard on the way!" Phoebe shouted down from the wheel house. "What's a cutter?" she asked.

"Gun boat. Send a message again. We're south of Pier Cove, heading toward them at full speed. Tell them to hurry!"

"Company's coming!" Fred almost chirped from the bow.

"Stand by! Mason, get on that light. When they fire the cannon, turn it on for a couple of seconds, and turn it off fast.

"All right everyone! Ready! Quiet! Keep quiet! And keep down!" Doctor Horace was listening for the sound of their engine, holding the megaphone up to his ear. It was still a good distance away but coming fast. "Let them get close this time. Wait. Wait! Now! Fire the cannon!"

Fred and Theo fired the second shot, this time sending a spray of ball bearings and bolts somewhere near the boat. Someone on the launch let out a yelp of pain, just as Mason turned on the light. It blinded them, and for a second the pilot looked like he was losing control and would flip the boat in a tight turn. He regained the wheel and pulled sharply to the left, racing out into the deep water some distance from the *Aurora*.

"You got someone behind you!" Gar shouted down at Doctor Horace.

He turned around as the figure stepped out of the shadows. "Why, Mrs. Smith. I was wondering when you would join us," he said with calmness that surprised even himself. He looked down at a brown paper package tied with string.

"How did you know I was aboard?" she demanded.

"Because my car was riding a little low on the way back from Ox-Bow. Nor did I see you leave the ship back in Saugatuck. I assume you're the reason for our evening's entertainment, aren't you?"

Her mouth was open in shock, and for a moment she was speechless. "It's me they're after. And this," she said, holding up her package.

He looked at her, then at the package. "That must be important."

"I'll tell you later," she said firmly.

"If there is a later, thanks to you." Horace growled at her. "You've put all of us in grave danger."

"It can't be helped. I want a spotlight on me. Now!" she commanded.

She had angered Horace faster and more intensely than anyone in the past few decades. Even Nitti's drunken visit wasn't nearly as infuriating. He was about to say something when she repeated. "Spotlight. Now". Her command was sharp.

Horace signalled for Gar to turn the portable search light in the wheel house onto the woman on the deck. She took the doctor's megaphone in one hand and held her package up in the other. She stood silently on the deck, waiting until she was sure she had the attention of the men in the outboard.

Slowly, very calmly, deliberately, and loudly, she shouted something to them. No one on the *Aurora* could understand what she was saying. Fred thought it was German. So did Theo. Phoebe and Gar were confused. Horace thought it was Polish or Russian.

Horace motioned for Gar to turn off the light. "Just what did you tell them?" he demanded of the woman.

"I told them to surrender immediately or I would drop this package into the water. They are to throw their guns over-board, turn off the motor, and put their hands up until we arrive."

"I see," he said quietly. He took back his megaphone. "Mason, see if those thugs are running the white flag up their flag pole."

Mason turned on the light, searched across the water, and found the boat.

A shot rang out. The light was hit and went dark.

"The stern light is knocked out of commission," he shouted.

"Well, they gave their answer. I don't think they're ready to give up and go home," Horace said quickly. "Ready everyone!"

He suddenly dashed into the library, pulled open the hidden compartment above the one where he kept his whiskey, and pulled out a glass bottle from a leather case. Without a word he dashed up to the bow. "Put this in the cannon," he said. He opened the bottle and carefully put a couple of large silvery metal blocks into his handkerchief and gingerly handed them to Theo. "As soon as they start coming this way, get ready to fire. Then reload."

He dashed back to the middle of the *Aurora*. "Quiet! Quiet! Listen!"

No one dared breathe loudly. "Here they come again! Get down woman!" he pulled Mrs. Smith to the deck.

"Fire!"

Once again the signal cannon barked, this time leaving a snowfall of purple fabric from what had once been Horace's handkerchief.

A few seconds later the water just in front of the launch geysered up with a muffled roar from beneath the surface, and a thickening plume of white smoke mushroomed over the water. A second or two later and it would have been directly under the four men. "Light two rockets, Harriet!" Horace shouted. "One after the other!" The second one followed the arch of the first, and exploded, this time filling the sky with a magnificent display of colors.

From the *Aurora*, even without his field glasses, Horace could see that the men in the boat were drenched, and the boat was out of control for a second time. And for the second time the man at the wheel fought to steady it before they roared away.

"What was that?" Harriet shouted at him.

"About a quarter pound of pure sodium," Horace laughed, jumping up and down and clapping his hands in glee. "That should give them something to think about."

"Where's the Coast Guard?" he shouted up at Phoebe.

"I think they're a couple of minutes away. But I haven't learned numbers yet," she wailed, almost in despair.

"Never mind that. Send a message. Tell them to watch for our signal!"

He turned to Harriet. "Keep firing those rockets so the Coast Guard can find us! One at a time, and pause until the light fades before you light the next one." Harriet waved, took a puff on the cigar to freshen the glow, coughed profusely, and lit the rockets one after another.

"That's all of them. Now what?" she yelled at him.

"You run up to the wheel house and bring down the flare gun and all the flares you find. And you," he said to Mrs. Smith, "go light off some of these lady fingers. Just a couple of them at a time. Pause and count, then another one. Let them think we're shooting at them!"

"Haven't you got any guns?" she demanded.

"Yeah. Two small pistols. And one without any shells left. I assume you want them alive, don't you?"

"Those firecrackers aren't going to do any good!" she snapped at him. He ignored her.

"Coast Guard's almost here. All we have to do is bluff them and hold them off a few more minutes. Do as you're told, woman. I don't know who you are or who you think you are, but I own this boat, and no mistake about it. You understand?"

Mrs. Smith didn't see the logic to it, but went to the rail and started lighting them. "They'll think they're a pistol!" Horace called after her.

"Now what?" Harriet asked.

Horace showed her how to open the breach and put in a flare, close it. "Just aim for the sky and fire it. Like this!"

He fired off the first flare. It shot up, and lit up the sky, the parachute slowing its descent, the light playing on the water. He handed the pistol back to her and watched as she pulled out the spent casing and reloaded.

"Not nobody look up!" Fred shouted. "The Boche can spot you a mile off." Horace rolled his eyes. Fred was living in the past, still fighting the last war.

The flare revealed that the four men in the boat were taking a different approach for their next attack. They circled wide behind the *Aurora*, this time coming along the port side along the shore. There was no time to turn the cannon around. And this time three of them were shooting, the bullets pinging against the hull, and one of them striking the metal ladder, ricocheting into the teak deck. They flew past the *Aurora*, heading straight past the bow.

Without thinking, Harriet reloaded the flare gun, aiming it at the boat, shouting at them, "No body shoots at my daughter! No one! Ever!"

"Shoot up, woman! Shoot up!" Horace shouted at her in anger. It was too late. She pulled the trigger and fired.

For a few seconds they watched as the flare trailed straight behind the outboard, then disappeared in the dark. Both of them thought it had hit the water and was extinguished. They didn't realize it flew between the men, and exploded under the deck in the bow. There were screams from the men. And more screams when the flare ignited the gasoline tanks. A violent explosion lifted the boat out of the water just as the men dived from it.

Horace and Harriet stood shoulder to shoulder, not certain they believed what they were watching. "Did I do that?" Harriet whispered, still in shock.

"You did," Horace could barely croak out.

"Oh, my God, I've killed them!" she moaned, then fainted. Horace barely caught her and lowered her to the deck.

"No, you didn't kill them, but you are a real Annie Oakley!" He held her against him. "You really are."

CHAPTER NINE

"Circle about and prepare to rescue the survivors," Horace managed to shout up to Gar. He realized he was shaking. The old captain pulled hard on the wheel, then signalled quarter speed down to the engine room. A few seconds later he pulled 'Stop Full' to let the *Aurora* drift closer.

"All hands to the port side to form a rescue party." Gar shouted.

Horace was helping Harriet to her feet to lead her to a deck chair. "Where's the pistol?" Mrs. Smith demanded. He handed the empty one to her.

Phoebe saw her mother and nearly tripped hurrying down the stairs. "Is Mother hurt?" she started crying.

"No, she's fine. Just fainted. She's going to be very proud of you. Help me get her to that chair." Horace said, nodding toward a recliner. Together they steadied Harriet as she shuffled forward.

"Another patient for you, nurse," he called to Clarice. "Fainted at the sight of blowing up a boat all on her own," Horace managed to laugh. Clarice came out of the library to attend to Harriet. "You stay with them, Phoebe. She'll want you the moment she feels better." He watched as mother and daughter embraced.

"I'll handle everything here," Clarice said. "What about the others?"

"I'll find out. I'll have Mrs. Garwood give you a hand if they're hurt."

Mrs. Smith was speaking to the four men as they clung tightly to the ropes lowered from the deck of the *Aurora*. She held the pistol up for them to see, warning them that she would shoot if they moved a muscle. At least that is what Horace thought she said. It was in the same foreign language as before.

"What did you tell them?" Horace demanded.

"I said that if they moved I would shoot to kill."

"Well, that should work," Theo answered, standing next to his brother.

They watched the Coast Guard cutter steam close to them, search-lights plying the water. A young man was standing behind a large machine gun mounted on the bow. Other officers and men had their pistols drawn, ready for action. The boat came alongside the *Aurora*.

"When you said to watch for your signal, I didn't think you meant we'd be seeing a Fourth of July fireworks display! Quite the show you folks put on for us. Lieutenant Thomas, US Coast Guard, here to assist. You want to tell us what is going on?"

Before Horace could answer, Mrs. Smith stepped in front of the lieutenant, pulling a badge from a jacket pocket. "I am Special Agent Winifred Smith with the US Attorney General's Office. These four are my prisoners. You are to take them aboard your vessel and transport them to your brig and hold them. I will be interrogating them later."

"Now listen lady...." the lieutenant interrupted.

"No, you listen. You will do as I say. You will take those four men and keep them in the brig until they are transported by a federal agent. I won't hesitate to speak to your superiors if you don't follow orders. Is that clear?" she snapped at them. "And see to it that no one knows that you have them until I return. No one, do you understand? Especially not the local police or sheriff. This is a federal arrest. Now, do as you are ordered." She stared down the officer until he finally ordered his men to get the four swimmers out of the water.

When Harriet had accidently fired a flare into the small launch and set it ablaze, the fire had lit up the library despite the heavy curtains. And, hearing the shouts and raised voices, as well as Harriet's wail of dismay, then Horace's summons, Clarice had rushed out of the room, forgetting all about her patient, Frank Nitti. While no one was noticing, he staggered out of the room and across the deck, to clear his head, resting on the starboard rail.

"Pretty good shooting, girlie," he snickered.

Horace turned around. "I thought I told you to keep him sedated," he whispered at Clarice.

"I thought he was out like a light," she whispered back.

"Yeah, pretty good shooting, girlie. Now, if you'd like to go to work for us down to Chicago, say, we'd pay you real good! We could use a girlie like you." He laughed in derision, smirking at her. In the light he looked like a rat with yellow teeth.

Harriet stood up, blood rushing through her brain, as she picked up the flare gun, opened the breach to put in a new shell, and came towards him. She stared at his eyes. Very quietly and deliberately she said, "I have waited ten years to do this. I don't know if you pulled the trigger that killed my husband or not, and right now that doesn't matter. I'm going to shoot this flare gun, point blank, and it will hit you in the chest and kill you. And because you are such a worthless piece of rubbish everyone here will say it was an accident. You think I'm a good shot? I don't know. Maybe I am. Maybe I just got lucky. But at this range I know I can't miss. And you know it, too!"

She raised the gun and pulled back the hammer just as Doctor Horace stepped up next to her. "That will do, Harriet," he said softly. "This is not something you want your daughter to see, and it's not something I want my granddaughter to see." He gently lifted her arm up, put his finger over hers and together they pulled the trigger. The flare streaked into the sky.

She turned to Horace, her eyes wide, her whole body shaking. "You know?"

"I've suspected as much for the last few days. You just confirmed it."

Harriet dropped the pistol as the two of them wrapped their arms around each other. They stood together for a few moments, Harriet sobbing and shaking, until he led her back to the chair. "Take care of your mother," he told Phoebe.

Doctor Horace slowly walked toward the stern, slipping into the shadows, then grasped the rail to steady himself. He was shaking violently, his mind racing through horrid night scenes from a decade before in France.

Gar saw him and helped him into the library. "A little nerve medicine, Doc," he said. Gar opened the cabinet and pulled out the bottle of whiskey. "A dram will do you a world of good right now." He opened the bottle and handed it to his boss, then took a large drink himself. "And me, too," he chuckled.

"You have no idea...." Doctor Horace started to say.

"Yeah, I do. Night like this brings it all back, don't it?"

The men took a second bump. They were both shaking less. "To the boys who didn't come home," Gar said sadly as he lifted his class.

Theo went over to the rail and stood next to Nitti. "Frankie, it's been quite the night. Ah, look at yourself. You wet your pants again.

Not been a good night for you, though, has it? Second time tonight. You don't smell so good, either." He sniffed the air. "Think you did more than wet your pants from the stench."

The gangster was shaking slightly, his face red, either from the booze or humiliation of being stared down by a woman.

"Listen, Frankie, let me help you out here. Best thing you can do is get yourself arrested for public intoxication and disorderly conduct. Couple of days in jail," Theo suggested.

"Nah, I'm going to go back to Saugatuck and take care of business!"

"That's not smart thinking, Frankie. You know better than that. Think straight. Think it through, careful like."

"Yeah, well, we got a good thing going there. Money just rolls in that party town!"

"Oh, I'm sure it does. But you go back there and before long everyone's going to know an old lady cold-cocked you with a frying pan 'cause you were so stinking drunk you didn't see it coming, and then you messed your pants like a little boy. You know, I think it was her that took your guns off you, too. The one in the holster and the one on your ankle. Imagine how people would laugh when they hear that! An old woman takes you down and then takes your pieces off you. And they'll know you messed your pants a second time when a girl gets the drop on you with a flare gun. They'll be laughing at you, Frankie, especially if you turn up stinking the way you do right now."

"Nobody laughs at Frank Nitti! Nobody. Not even Snarky, and he's bigger than the whole government and the President put together. I'm Frank Nitti, and you remember that!"

"Settle down and think this through. You go back there and they'll know the whole story. Maybe they won't laugh at you to your face, but behind your back. They won't treat you with respect. You want to be treated with respect, don't you, Frank?" Theo asked.

"Everyone respects Frank Nitti!" he repeated. "I'm Frank Nitti!"

"Well, they won't. Trust me. And before long, word will get back to Capone and to the other fellows in your organization how people are laughing at you, and them. Maybe Capone will figure you need to go because you're weak. Or maybe some young gun will think if he takes you out he moves up. You think about that?"

The gangster was silent. "Yeah, I see your point. Maybe I lay low for a while."

"That's the smart thinking Frank Nitti I know!" Theo said. "Lay low a long time. You let those fellows arrest you. They'll keep you safe, get you a fresh suit, fix you up. Give you a chance to get your story straight about how the feds locked you up. They'll respect you that way. Capone, all of them. Real badge of honor, getting arrested while taking care of business."

Nitti nodded his head in agreement.

"Say, there's another thing, Frankie. You and your business associates ought to stay out of our town, too. I mean, you know how it is, Clarice and Horace, Fred, the rest of them, they all saw you get taken down by a frying pan and how you messed up your pants. And then that young lady getting the drop on you. I don't know that Horace and I can keep them from talking back to home. Why don't you find yourself a new doctor, somewhere far away? Think that'd be smart?"

"Yeah, yeah, yeah. You're talking straight, Doc."

"This one goes to the county jail. Drunk and disorderly, and using uncouth language in front of a woman," Theo said.

"He got a name?" the lieutenant asked.

"I'm Frank Nitti! That's who I am! You got it? Frank Nitti!" he roared in defiance.

"Sure you are, fella, and I'm the Kaiser." He motioned for two of his men to help get Nitti off the *Aurora* and onto their cutter.

Theo was quite pleased with himself. With a bit of luck, that would be the end of dealing with Nitti and Capone in Saugatuck and back home.

"I believe you have a lot of explaining to do, Miss," Horace said firmly.

"I don't believe I need to explain anything about a government investigation," she shot back at him.

"That's where we disagree. So, unless you want to swim, walk, or hitchhike back to Saugatuck...."

She glared at him in fury. "Very well." She led them into the library, then demanded to know how soon they would be sailing.

"When you explain and answer our questions," Horace said.

She waited until everyone was seated, not registering any surprise that Harriet and Horace were sitting closely together, and Phoebe on his lap, with Gar's steel helmet now on her lap. Mrs. Smith looked around the room, teasing them with a dramatic long pause to make certain they were all listening and focused on her.

"As I am sure you understand by now, I am a federal agent with the Department of Justice. So was my late partner. We were made aware of a forgery ring in the Chicago area. At first we thought it was one of the mobsters, Banion, Capone, Moran. Take your pick. But this isn't their regular line of work, what we in the department call, 'modus operandi'. We eventually traced it down to some Poles. Reds. Red Poles."

"You mean, like Bolshies?" Clarice asked.

"Polish Bolsheviks, yes. They were engraving plates to forge bonds in the name of the Polish national government. You may recall a few years ago there was a coup in Poland, and Lenin, and then Trotsky and Stalin saw a chance. A chance to destabilize the government and conquer it, and make a lot of money at the same time. They wanted the land back like it was before the war. American money to spread communism around the world. By selling phony bonds.

"The front plate was done in Chicago, and we've had it under surveillance. A few weeks ago, the four men you encountered tonight came up here, thinking they could blend in with the other Poles at that church camp, and do their work at Ox-Bow. Fred and I were ordered to come up here in disguise...."

"Just a minute," Harriet interrupted. "You can't just waltz your way into the pulpit of an Episcopal Church. I'll admit we're a little casual, at least in Saugatuck, but...."

"I will only tell you that Mr. Barbour was persuaded by Washington to cooperate, shall we say, with our investigation. Fred kept watch in town; I watched them at the camp, pretending to be an art student."

"The worst I've ever seen," Harriet whispered under her breath. Mrs. Smith ignored the slight.

"The last day of classes, I finished my painting. The same size as their engraving plate. Fred distracted them just long enough for me to switch my painting and their plate. I put the plate in the car and Fred drove back.

"At the bottom of the hill there is an old stump and some brush. Fred dropped the plate there, hiding it in plain sight under some leaves and twigs, and then went to the rectory. The plan was for me to stay at the camp, be obvious, and get a ride back. Sooner or later the forgers would discover what I had done and we would spring the trap."

"But it didn't work that way, did it?" Horace asked.

"No. Doctor Mason delayed me by not being ready in time. The fellows saw me get in his car and followed on foot and the ferry, so when we got back into town, I had to lose them for a while in the crowds. I thought that if they didn't find their plate at the church house they'd think Doctor Mason had it, and when they discovered he didn't have it, they'd circle back."

"Which is how Fred got himself killed," Horace said with a twinge of disgust.

"A casualty of war," she said flatly, without emotion.

"You nearly made me one, too!" Dr. Mason snapped.

The agent ignored him and continued, "When I realized our plan was falling apart, I had to improvise. I had to get back to the camp to get the plate and secure it. I spotted some young people having a petting party on the river bank, went past them, and walked straight into the water. I got out a ways, slipped under and floated past some houses. Once I got my bearings I swam to shore, retrieved the plate, and hid out.

"Where? I heard the camp was searched seven ways to Sunday!" Doctor Mason said.

"In what you call your hidey-hole," the agent smiled.

"Yeah? Well, how'd you get in? The doors are locked from the outside. Padlocks."

The agent snorted. Your shack is on pilings. I crawled underneath the house and cut through the chicken wire fence and opened the trap door. I saw it when I came by your place. By the way, the police chief wasn't smart enough to figure it out, but the girl was. Your daughter kept me well supplied with some fruit and cookies." She looked at Phoebe and then Harriet. "And your security at that camp is lacking. I helped myself to the ice box and pantry late at night."

Harriet and all of the adults turned to look at Phoebe, wondering how she had figured it out.

"Well, we all knew how to get in! Just like in the cave under that big house up on the hill, or the hidden door to the basement of All Saints. And the hidey-hole under the hardware store!" Phoebe said brightly. "And there is another one under the Crow Bar!" She seemed extremely proud of herself for outsmarting the police chief and all the other adults. She looked up at her mother. Harriet was not impressed.

"You could have been killed!" her mother gasped.

"But I wasn't, was I, Mother?" she giggled.

"Which probably explains how you got from Mason's cabin and on to my boat," Horace asked. "I hope the trunk of my car wasn't too comfortable for you. I assume you didn't latch it so you could get out."

"Yes. Thanks to Phoebe and you."

"And the grip with the Russian money and that medal made into a tie clasp?" Horace asked.

"Ah, that. Well, Fred had been with the American Embassy as a military attaché before the war, and then later with the Expeditionary Force that went to Russia at the end of the war. He speaks, well, spoke, fluent Russian, so he was a translator. I won't say how he came across the money, but it helps establish our bona fides with the Mensheviks.

"Mens mensa, mens what?" Theo asked.

"White Russians, loyal to the Romanovs, enemies of the Reds. It's worthless paper now, but their eyes light up when they see it. It reminds of them of the old country.

"As for the Saint Stanislaus medal and tie, it's a pass code between the members of the Polar Bear Battalion - Saint Stanislaus over the Bolo - the bolo tie." She seemed quite pleased divulging that information.

"So Fred and I heard up in Holland when we had an army reunion," Theo said. He delighted in deflating the agent of her little gem of wisdom.

Mrs. Smith looked surprised that they were ahead of her on that point.

"So to cut to the chase scene as they say in the Tom Mix picture shows, you got on my boat to flush out the Bolos, and put all of us in great danger," Horace retorted angrily. "My brother and his wife, my employees, and my guests. Is that correct?"

"It was a calculated risk in the war," she replied firmly.

"War? What war?" Horace asked.

"The war to preserve our way of life against the Russians, the Reds, the Wobblies. All of them! You were part of the war effort! Fred and I want to restore the Romanovs to their rightful station."

"And you're telling me the federal government is behind this?" Clarice asked. "I can't believe it!"

Again, the agent ignored a direct question.

"I see. And just how do you think you're going to keep this from Callie and out of the newspapers? Horace demanded.

"I am sure they will be persuaded to cooperate," she answered smugly. "Let's just say that it will be in their best interests to do so."

Horace moved Phoebe to her mother's lap and stalked out of the library to put some distance between himself and Mrs. Smith. He was furious with her. She'd risked their lives, playing fast and easy with all of them. And on top of that, trying to topple the Russian government, even if they were Reds. Pure audacity.

He stared out the water, dark now, and somehow it relaxed him. He returned a few minutes later. "Gar, start up the engines and take us back to Saugatuck. I would like to get our stowaway back on shore!" He left again, the captain close behind as they went out on the deck.

"That won't be necessary. The cutter is still close by. Signal them to return. I'll accompany my prisoners," Mrs Smith commanded.

"Gar, you think you can get us down the channel to Saugatuck safely?" he asked, his temper calmed. The two of them watched the cutter return. "I doubt anyone will be shooting at us this time."

"It's a cake-walk. They didn't get the front search light. If somebody will get up on that light, I'll get home safe and sound, right between the reds and greens."

"Good man. And thank you for getting us through this one safe and sound."

"Just like old times, huh, boss? Fred, too. Did you hear him? Thought he was still fighting the Germans."

"And may we never see them again!"

"Memories sure do last, don't they, boss?"

Doctor Horace's face muscles tightened, and he wandered back into the shadows near the stern.

"I followed the smoke. James said you smoked a pipe when you were thinking. I told you that, didn't I? Is that when you knew?" Harriet asked quietly.

"Before then, really. I had an idea when I first saw Phoebe. She looks a bit like my other granddaughter. Then when you mentioned the pipe. And tonight...." his voice trailed off.

"What happened between you two, if you don't mind me asking?" she asked quietly.

"James and I were more than father and son; the best of friends. Well, after he got a bit older and, to be honest, more interesting. I thought he'd follow me into medicine, like Theo and I followed our father. He was at Northwestern studying biology when the war broke out. I couldn't see him doing surgery, but still, a doctor. He'd have been a top flight pathologist. When war broke out in 1914, like a lot of young men he got caught up in Theodore Roosevelt's war hawking, and joined the SATC."

"SATC?"

"Student Army Training Corp. James called it Safe At the College. He quit, enlisted, and got hooked up with Colonel Robert McCormick - First Battery, Fifth Field Artillery - and saw action at Cantigny. He admired McCormick so much he decided to become a writer, and that hurt, as you can imagine. A writer instead of a physician. McCormick hired him for the Tribune. Broke my heart, but it's what he wanted to do at the time. And then he said he'd fallen for some woman and wanted to get married. You?"

"Me," she said.

"I could tell I was getting squeezed out, pushed aside. It is what all young men should do, perhaps, but... I didn't take it very well. That was bad enough, and I made it worse, trying too hard to win him back. After the war, I wanted things to go back the way they used to be. He wouldn't forgive me for not getting home in time for his mother and sister's funeral. I couldn't have gotten there any faster if I had tried, and considering it was during the Spanish Flu epidemic, they couldn't delay the burial. It wasn't really my fault, but I can't blame him for getting hurt. All things together, we both took it hard, all of it, and we had a falling out. A bad one. I never knew he got married. Not until later.

"Anyway, after a while, Theo talked me into going to Tokyo for a conference. He said maybe getting away and some distance would help. He meant well; he always does. Knowing my brother and Clarice, they were planning on a come-to-Jesus meeting with James. That didn't happen. About a day out of San Francisco I got a telegram that he'd been killed. We couldn't turn around, so we went to Hawaii and I turned around on the next boat back to the States, but by then....." He reached for the handkerchief in his coat pocket, but it was gone. He'd used it in the cannon earlier. He used the back of his hand to remove a tear.

"I'm sorry, Harriet. I am so, so sorry. You've got a wonderful daughter. You shouldn't have gotten caught up in our family's squabble."

"And you've got a wonderful granddaughter. But she can be a handful at times," she laughed for a second.

"A wonderful granddaughter," he whispered. "And a wonderful daughter-in-law. You still are, you know. If you want to be."

They stood at the rail, looking at the water behind them. "And James? No one ever told me how it happened. I suppose they wanted to protect me," he barely whispered. "Truth is, I couldn't bear to find out."

"You probably know he got a job at the City Desk for all the papers in Chicago. One afternoon there was a call about a police raid so he went to report on it. There was a shoot out, and....." her voice trailed off. The silence of the night was broken only by the sound of the water. Harriet didn't need to explain that her husband had been caught in the crossfire.

"And afterwards you reverted back to your maiden name?" Horace asked.

"I did, and it had nothing to do with you. Really. Truly, nothing to do with you. Or your family. There were never any hard feelings. My mother was widowed young, too. I saw how she coped alone, and James always encouraged me to be independent. Maybe I was wrong and foolish, but I didn't want people asking if I was related to the Balfour doctors. So, I went back to being Harriet Walters and we moved up here for a fresh start. Disappointed in me for my decisions?"

"Surprisingly, no. No, I'm not. I admire you for it. And you certainly taught Phoebe to be independent," he smiled.

"Maybe too independent, spunky, feisty, and forward," she forced a slight laugh.

Doctor Horace put his arm around his daughter-in-law's shoulder and gave her a slight hug.

The *Aurora* tied up a little after midnight, and Horace walked Harriet and Phoebe back home. The girl was asleep on his shoulder.

"Will we see you again?" Harriet finally asked, half afraid of his answer.

CHAPTER TEN

Right after sunrise Gar pulled on the whistle cord, then signalled the engine room to set off, quarter speed ahead. She made a magnificent sight, a plume of black smoke belched from the two stacks, then a steady stream as her paddle wheels steadily beat against the water. She made her way down the Kalamazoo River. Years later, people would always remember the *Aurora*. The graceful old lady, her white hull, teak and mahogany wood, and those big red paddle wheels.

"We've missed her!" a young voice wailed. "She's gone! He's gone! I didn't get to say goodbye. What if I don't ever see him again?" She began to sob. All that was left was a trail of blackish-grey smoke fading further down the river where it bends.

"I know dear. Doctor Horace couldn't stay here forever and ever, but he'll be back. He promised, and I promise he'll be back! You'll see." The girl was sobbing; the woman with her dabbing a handkerchief at her eyes, as they stood on the dock.

They didn't hear the soft steps behind them. "Yes, and I think the man who owns her was hoping to buy some posies this morning. Or, hire a tour-guide to show him around town."

The girl wheeled around and rushed toward him. "Grandpa!"

When the hugs subsided and the tears were brushed from their cheeks, Harriet asked. "You didn't leave?"

"No. I decided to stay on for a while. You see, yesterday afternoon I went over to the drug store to have a chocolate phosphate.

You ever have their chocolate phosphates? Never had a better one. Best soda fountain I've ever enjoyed. You've been holding out on me, young lady. Anyway, I was talking to the fellow who owns the place, and he said that your regular town doc is gone on a study tour. Some place called Eccles. Ever hear of it? I guess they've got a hospital there that's supposed to be pretty good. Apparently, he wanted to see a new technique that a Doctor Theodore Balfour is doing. Then he's going up north to do a little fishing. Won't be back until mid-September."

"But Theo, has been here all this time," Harriet said.

"I think your doctor found that out the hard way when he got there. I understand from my secretary he was a little sore about it, too. I sent him a telegram to tell him that Theo would be on the night train out of Chicago today and should be back to the hospital by tomorrow morning. And, that I wanted to make it up to him....." He paused, then smiled broadly.

"So, I'm filling in until then. Told him to stay until the end of summer if he wants to."

"And you'll be happy stitching up cuts and putting salve on scrapes and setting a few bones?" Harriet asked a bit warily.

"You know, I think I will," he said slowly and thoughtfully. "It'll remind me of when I hung out my shingle fifty some years ago. It's good to remember where you come from. Keeps a man humble, and that's important. I learned that lesson the past few days. That, and about families and loved ones. You can't just walk in and out of their lives. Besides, I figure that since Nitti won't be using his room, they'd welcome a new guest at the Butler Hotel."

"But Saugatuck isn't very exciting, not for you!" Harriet objected.

"Now, that's where you are wrong. Just lively enough to satisfy me, what with you two here. And say, did I ever tell you I was licensed by the Bishop back home to be a Lay Reader? If doctoring doesn't keep me busy I can always take up preaching," he laughed.

"And then you could stay in the church house!" Phoebe cheered. And I could come and see you every day and cook for you and everything, couldn't I, Grandpa?

"Really? Can you cook?" he asked. "Maybe I might finally have some whitefish."

"Welllllll... not yet, but I could practice, just like doctors practice medicine!"

"Add tummy aches to your list of things to cure. Starting with your own," Harriet giggled.

"Definitely lively enough for me," Horace said.

"Is it a deal?" Phoebe asked.

"Deal!" Horace and Phoebe looked at each other, burst out in big smiles, and in unison spit in to their right palm and smashed their left fist in it. Harriet shook her head in mock disgust, and joined them in their ritual.

"Deal," she laughed.

The three of them walked along Water Street to Harriet and Phoebe's home. "You know, ladies, I see why you like it here. Fact is, I've almost come to believe that a day away from Saugatuck is a day wasted."

AUTHOR'S NOTES

This is the place where I have to write the legal disclaimer that all the characters are fiction and there are absolutely, positively, definitely no similarities between the quick and the dead.

There. Written. Mostly it applies. There are some bits and pieces of the truth, however.

The places are real: especially the Sand Bar, Big Pavilion, Saugatuck Drug Store, All Saints' Episcopal Church, Ox-Bow, the Presbyterian Camp, and Saugatuck. All of them are still around except the Big Pavilion which burned, and the Presbyterian Camp which closed down. Years later the little bungalow at All Saints' was moved to make room for the Parish Hall. The Crow Bar eventually became Coral Gables after the Johnson family bought it, but they kept the original name over the lounge. It's a good place for whitefish, by the way.

Some of the people, especially the fellows at the Sand Bar – Billy, Thomas, Al, Hack, and Old Chris – are, or were real. The first three are still very much alive, and you can probably find them having coffee every morning; the latter two have passed away. And, just in case you're curious, Thomas did write the song mentioned in the beginning.

There was a telephone operator by the name of "Bobbie" but I don't know if she was asking, "Number, please?" when this story took place. It might have been before her time.

Frank Nitti, the enforcer for the Chicago Outfit, was a real person, but I don't know that he was ever in town. There are so many stories about Big Al and his cronies being in western Michigan that they wouldn't have had time to get any gangster work done in Chicago. And a couple of minor characters were real – Trix and Ollie, both musicians. Trix played for the NBC orchestra, and later became a music professor at DePaul University in Chicago. Oliver Anderson had an early jazz band when he was a Boy Scout, and it was called the Black Hawk Orchestra, out of Aurora, Illinois. He was the leader and drummer. Both of them were my uncles. And Doctor Mason did exist, and did build a cottage at Ox-Bow which is still in use during the summer season. Everything else about him in this is complete fiction.

Courtney Barbour is mentioned a couple of times, and he was a real person who lived in Chicago and spent his summers here. But that business about him being coerced into helping cover things up is pure fiction. The man was devout and a straight-arrow.

Sylvia, Jane, and Cora, the harbour master, were real. All of them great people, and much beloved in our community.

As for everyone else, that's another matter. If you can find some similarity between a real person, dead or alive, that's your look out. There isn't one, intentional or coincidental, and if you think there is, that's a figment of your imagination.

Well, except for Phoebe, and the young woman who was the inspiration for her told me it was quite all right to go forward and have fun. She read the manuscript and said it was "jake with me".

As for the murder of the ersatz Episcopal minister, that is just pure unadulterated fiction. It never happened. There is no truth to it, what-so-ever. Pure and simple, no messing. One long tall tale.

Not that I haven't been having a bit of fun with planting a few ideas. When I first started on this project a few years ago I asked people if they had ever heard about the cover-up of the Episcopal minister who was murdered. No one had, of course, but after a year or so a few people said that they thought they had heard something about it, but didn't know any details. A few of them thought I ought to do a little research and write the history of the event.

Just to make it clear again: The murder is pure fiction, bunkum, a tall tale.

Then again, the history of All Saints' Church during that time is a bit sketchy, and despite my research, I cannot find each and every copy of the *Commercial Record* newspaper from that era.

The whole idea for this tall tale came into meaning primarily on the swing in the porch of the Old Inn at Ox-Bow. My wife is an artist and takes classes there every year. In addition, we go out for their Friday Open House programmes during the summer. After a while I generally camp out on the swing and stare across the meadow and lagoon. Sometimes I have a long stretch of waiting which I don't mind. Really long stretches of cooling my heels when she finds something interesting.

One final note about the last sentence in the book. It's a tip of the hat to my good friend, former mayor, and all round good fellow, Henry Van Singel. He always said, "A day away from Saugatuck is a day wasted" and claimed that he was the first to say it. I'm not so certain about that. I think I said it first and he borrowed it when he ran for City Council. Not that accuracy of facts matters when there is a story that can be told.

And that one sentence is perhaps the only bona fide, genuine, absolutely true and no mistake about it part of the book: A day away from Saugatuck is a day wasted.

— G Corwin Stoppel

36429027R00106

Made in the USA
San Bernardino, CA
22 July 2016